MW00885213

Coin

by J. B. Hardt

Acknowledgments

Heather, thank you for your continued support and input. This book wouldn't be possible without you. Ellie, thanks for your ability and efforts to help me tell the story I wanted to tell. Ben, thank you for your great advice. And, finally, Isabelle, thank you for pushing this story into its final form.

I would also like to acknowledge nanowrimo.org for getting the story out of me so quickly.

Departure.

"I love you."

Only silence answered Gideon's endearment. He pulled the phone away from his ear and frowned at the lock screen's confirmation that the call with his wife had ended without a response. *Did she hang up on me? Is she still mad?*

Gideon could be reading too much into it. Maybe Janna's battery died. She'd forgotten to put it on the charger last night. At least, that's what she had said and that's why it wasn't strange that her battery would die in the early afternoon.

"We're closing up soon." The bartender said in a throaty Arabic accent. He tossed his bar towel over his shoulder and raised his chin. "Would you like another, sir?"

A quick glance at the clock over the bar showed twenty 'til nine. "Sure." Gideon slammed the last of his scotch and pushed the glass toward the young local man. "Scotch. Neat."

Did the guy judge him for drinking? Nobody really partook in this region, but they did sell it in hotel bars, like this one, and a few other places that catered to the west. Did it matter what a stranger thought of him? Janna had lectured Gideon about drinking too much. That mattered.

Rubbing his hands over his face, Gideon exhaled through his fingers and groaned. He glanced around, hoping no one witnessed his frustration. Only one other man patronized the bar a few stools down. When Gideon met the man's gaze, the man said, "Women can be troubling, yes?" in a heavy accent. *Russian? Everyone here speaks so many languages. I only speak American.*

Gideon looked the man over. Desert khakis, a matching shirt, black boots, and a brown leather jacket, faded and cracked, screamed Russian military, but what did Gideon know? He'd only seen movies, and this was his first trip outside of North America, let alone to the Middle East.

"You don't have to tell me your woman troubles. I see them on your face. Only a woman could cause such anguish." The Russian sipped at a clear liquid. Gideon's bias assumed it to be vodka.

A Tuesday night resembled a Wednesday back in the states, so not a lot of people frequented any place, especially not one like this. Gideon propped an elbow at the bar, leaned on his hand, and looked at the man's profile. With his tanned, cracked face, the Russian must have spent years in the sun. Yet the cracks didn't pervade as much as the wrinkles that frequented Gideon's face. The man could have been the same age as Gideon but looked like he had taken a much healthier path in life. The drinking, poor diet, lack of exercise, and bad genetics had taken a toll on Gideon's body in the forty years he'd occupied it. The Russian's height and frame seemed similar enough to Gideon's. With the right discipline and motivation, Gideon convinced himself that he could look the same.

"My wife barks at me more than the dog," the Russian said before draining his drink. The stranger pointed a finger at the bartender, who nodded in return. "And another drink for my friend," the Russian added.

"Oh." Gideon glanced down at his untouched drink. "I don't think I should have another. I have a full one and they're closing soon."

"No." The man gave a stern look to the bartender and wagged a finger at him. "You will not close."

"Of course not, sir. We can stay open a little longer."

"See. No problem." The Russian smirked at Gideon.

"Well . . .." Gideon licked his lips, then pressed the glass against them and downed a quick drink. "Why not?" It didn't even burn going down. He'd had too many already.

"Was your wife, uh girlfriend, barking at you just now?"

"Huh?" Gideon shook his head. "No. I wish. She doesn't say much of anything these days."

"That sounds like my dream, friend." The Russian laughed and moved down the bar to sit next to Gideon. "Gahf. Gahf. When will you return? Yap. Yap. Yap. Send me more money." The Russian laughed some more.

"The money isn't a problem. This job covers that." Gideon smiled. "She doesn't get it though. She didn't want me to come here. Thinks it's dangerous, but it's not anymore. I *told* her that, but she won't listen."

"It is safe. This place is paradise, thanks to your people." The Russian gripped Gideon's shoulder. "American, right?"

"Yeah. I'm from Nebraska, but I'm not sure this place is safe thanks to America." Gideon took a sip. "But it is safe now. Otherwise, I wouldn't be here consulting about a nuclear reactor."

"Oooh." The Russian didn't hide his surprise. "So, the world isn't scared about them making nuclear bomb?"

"That's why *I'm* here." Gideon raised an eyebrow while the Russian patiently awaited a response. "I'm not bragging when I say it, but I'm the guy these companies go to when they need help with the software that runs modern reactors. Russia, my apologies, is behind in this regard, but the rest of the world has moved past simple manufacturing systems."

"Russia?" The Russian tilted his head.

"Your country?" Gideon asked.

"I'm Croatian." The Russian . . . the *Croatian* said. He laughed. "You Americans."

"I know." Gideon chuckled uncomfortably. "I'm sorry. I'm Gideon. What's your name?"

"Yuri," the Croatian said flatly. "I believe my father may have been in love with Russia."

Genuine laughter broke the silence that followed his admission.

Gideon wiped away a tear. The laugh did him good. "Yuri. That's very Russian."

"I know." Yuri's laughter faded. "My friends tease me all the time."

"I bet. Like the KGB spy everyone looked for in that old Kevin Costner movie," Gideon said.

Yuri's eyes bulged, then narrowed as he fiddled with his drink. "I've never heard of that one. I believe I was named in honor of Yuri Gagarin, the first man in space."

"Yeah." Gideon raised his glass to toast. "To Yuri Gagarin and my new friend Yuri."

Yuri tapped Gideon's glass with his own, and the two men sipped their drinks.

"So, your wife barks at you?" Gideon asked.

"Constantly." Yuri finished his drink and pointed at the bartender who began making him a new one.

Gideon finished his first scotch and pulled the second one closer. "It's not that my wife doesn't talk. She's just so short with me." Gideon lifted his drink in front of his face. "I think—" he swished the drink around in his glass"—I think she's going to leave me."

"Kids?" Yuri asked.

"A daughter."

"Much more difficult. The leaving."

"Yes. She's eleven. Millie. She's named after my wife's great grandmother, Millicent."

"I don't have children, but I've always wanted a daughter." Yuri stared into his drink. "A daughter would be amazing. You are lucky man."

Gideon unlocked his phone and showed Yuri his favorite picture of Millie. Relatively recent, at the end of winter in Nebraska, Millie, dressed for hiking, covered in dirt and leaves, held a small box above her head. Every bit as beautiful as her mother, Millie chose to wear her dark brown hair short and refrained from wearing makeup even though other girls her age had already begun to.

Gideon loved that Millie clung to her childhood and wasn't in a hurry to grow up. The idea of her growing up caused Gideon's heart to quicken.

"What is she holding?" Yuri asked.

"Oh. That's a geocache box."

Yuri's brows squeezed together tightly.

"People hide caches in cities and forests, really all over. They upload the GPS coordinates to the Internet and then other people go find them, sign the log, and sometimes there's stuff in there you can swap out." Gideon brought up his tracking page on his phone. "Look at all the ones Millie and I have found together all over the U.S."

"That seems like good fun." Yuri raised his drink. "And you a good father."

"Thank you, Yuri." Gideon spun his drink slowly on the table and reviewed the geocache map. Most of their finds were well over two years old. "I used to be. I don't even know who took that picture of her. It's been a long time since we went out together. We'll get out again soon. Well, maybe, but even Millie hasn't had much to say to me since I left for here."

"It sounds like your work here must be important. They will understand when you return." Yuri looked forward.

"It is important." Gideon turned his head toward his new friend. "I'm good at what I do, and I understand these modern systems. Not only did I design most of the control software, but I'm also the guy that goes onsite to ensure they're implemented properly. Plus, I've invented safety systems that guarantee the most dangerous pieces stay out of the hands of evildoers." Gideon emphasized the last word with air quotes.

"I am sure I would not understand," Yuri said.

"It's not that hard, but a lot of people think the details are confusing." Gideon drank some more of his scotch. "I personally think anyone could do what I do. It's just that nobody has the passion I do for this stuff. If it's something people don't like, they tend to not understand it, and in the case of software and hardware engineering, people deem it hard." Gideon shrugged. "The ten-thousand-foot view of it is that usable fuel and waste is secured through distribution and locking cages that can only be used for their intended purpose. A bad actor would have a better chance launching America's nuclear arsenal than getting ahold of any bomb making materials from these systems." Gideon raised his drink to Yuri. "It's safe."

"That is good to know." Yuri raised his glass in return. "But it's not much like politicians to put their trust in things which they have no understanding."

Gideon scrunched his lips and nodded. "True. Even the ones that have seen plutonium neutralized have their doubts, but this is happening. My company isn't even the main contractor, and we've already received a lofty payment up front. Which is why I'm here in person and not on the phone."

Finishing his drink, Yuri pointed at the bartender again, but the bartender did not move.

"I really must be closing," the bartender said and placed a paper bill between Yuri and Gideon.

Yuri's face flushed with anger.

"It's for the best." Gideon removed his wallet and laid his credit card next to the bill. "I've probably had too much to drink as it is."

"No." Yuri grabbed the bill. "I can't let you pay. This is my gift."

"I have an expense account." Gideon smiled and pushed his card toward the bartender, then stood up and finished his scotch.

Yuri stood as well, placing a hand on Gideon's shoulder. "I know another place that doesn't ever close. Let us go there and talk more about our troublesome women." Yuri's wide eyes implored. "I haven't yet told you the worst of what my wife says to me."

Gideon flattened his lips and nodded curtly. "Okay. I can do one more."

"Yes," Yuri said, slapping Gideon's shoulder. "One more drink. Ha ha."

While Yuri headed for the front door, Gideon finished paying and followed. The cool nighttime early spring air chased Gideons hands into his pockets while he caught up to his new friend. The street remained empty and quiet, save for one noisy vehicle somewhere behind them.

"Is it far, Yuri?" Gideon asked.

"No. No. Not far." Yuri looked around the street as if he were searching for the next bar. "Your Yana. Does she like to drink with you?"

"It's Janna, and no she doesn't. She says I get mean. I'm not mean." Gideon laughed. "I'm glad I met you, Yuri. It will be nice having a drinking buddy."

Slowing his pace, Yuri nodded and smiled. "That would have been nice, Gideon."

The noisy vehicle came up fast behind Gideon, grabbing his attention. A beat up, old, windowless, white van pulled up to the curb. Its tires squealed when it came to a stop. The side door screeched open, revealing several men wearing all black and full head scarves concealing their identities. Gideon sprang back, but Yuri pushed him into their waiting arms.

Resurrection.

The last six months had been a blur. Was I taken off the street? Had I really been held captive for six months? None of it seemed real. My mind bounced around. I had trouble getting a grasp on who I was. I couldn't say where the slacks and shirt I wore came from. I wiggled my toes in brand new shoes. The shoes were nice, but who picked them out? They were on the bed in the hotel. Weren't they? No. *Maybe.*

I shook my head. The lights. The dark. The beatings. The questions. The constant stupid questions. Who won the last World Series? What was your college roommate's name? Who was the twenty-fifth president? They had said I would die there if I didn't answer correctly. Then they snuck in the same difficult question. How do you remove the uranium without rendering it inert? They never liked my answer and threw me back into my pitch-black cell like garbage—after another beating, of course.

The limousine stopped on the tarmac. I stared out the window at the nearly two dozen people gathered to hear me speak. I shuddered and repeated the mantra in my head that kept me sane in what seemed like weeks at a time in solitary.

I am Gideon Mossert. Husband to Janna. Father to Millie. I'm going to keep on living. I live for them.

The world outside the car seemed fake, my existence a dream. They stole who I was. I covered my face with my hands and choked out the muffled cries that I couldn't hold in. What remained of me? *Me?*

A hand touched my arm, and I jerked away, startled by the touch. *That's right. I'm not alone. Keep it together.*

"Gideon. It's okay." Laura Sauvy, Vice President of Public Relations for my company, Bright Futures, held a steady palm toward me. "You've been through a lot, but it's over now. You're safe now."

Next to Laura, sat Mr. Spencer, who identified himself as special advisor to the White House. He didn't offer a first name and he didn't say much, but he nodded a lot and seemed to have a permanent smirk on his young face. His mouse brown hair and standard issue government face betrayed nothing about his thoughts. Unlike me, he likely pulled his wardrobe out of a closet full of identical nondescript black suits, white shirts, red ties, and dark sunglasses that stereotyped him as a spook from a movie, but this wasn't a movie. He just wanted to make sure I didn't say anything I wasn't supposed to. How could I? I didn't know anything.

"Everything is okay, Gideon," Laura said.

"That's what the shrink that you made me see says," I bit back.

I thought I understood these people, but I didn't. What could I learn about someone from small talk or by the look of them? Still, the sum of Laura's words and exterior equaled career executive. She had medium length light brown hair with blonde highlights, pulled into a high ponytail. Her jacket and matching skirt, cut just above the knees, looked expensive with not a wrinkle in sight and even in the dark of the limousine interior, her bright white shirt radiated with pristine elegance.

I glanced down my nose at her sensible, likely expensive tan heels. A classy golden necklace with a matching bracelet completed her calculated, simple, yet elegant wardrobe. No rings on her fingers. No, that would be tacky for someone married to their job. The career executive's words echoed in my mind. *Everything is okay.*

"Is it okay?" I mumbled to myself. "I can do it. I want to help."

"Good Gideon. I think that's best for everyone."

"Tell me." I gritted my teeth at the small horde of reporters who shifted their microphones and cameras in my direction. "What took you so long to get me?"

"We paid the ransom immediately," Laura said, her body rigid and unyielding.

Mr. Spencer smirked, or he didn't. It was hard to tell.

Laura licked her lips. "They took their time releasing you."

"Took their time." My raised voice echoed off the interior of the limo. I spoke in a more reasonable tone. "I'm sorry. Tell me again what you want me to say."

I didn't listen to her, even though I'd asked. Only the cadence of her rehearsed words reached my ears like a song as the words flowed up and down. Laura's speaking voice had been perfected throughout her career for certain.

Husband to Janna. Father to Millie. They need me.

Silence snapped me out of my daze. Laura and Spencer stared at me.

"I don't recall what happened that night six months ago. It's all a blur, just like my time in captivity."

Laura nodded approvingly and Mr. Spencer remained unreadable. Amazingly the truth met their expectations.

"I'm just thankful to be alive, and I can't wait to see my wife and daughter again."

"Perfect." Laura held up her phone, apparently looking at her notes. "And if someone goes off script and asks about your work on the reactor?"

"Would they dare?" My nostrils flared. "My captors didn't ask about the reactor. They only took me for the ransom."

"This should all go well, Gideon. It would have been better if your family had made the trip, but I don't believe there will be any problems and then we'll all be back on schedule."

I squinted my eyes at the insensitive woman. *If my family had made the trip. Yeah. I would have liked that too.* Why weren't they here? I had a lot of work to do, repairing my relationship with my wife and daughter. Shaking my head, I turned and stared back out the window.

Typical. The company representative only sees the public image impact to them and not my personal pain from Janna and Millie's absence.

Corporations are people, but all these people cared about was making money. The truth? I did want to get back to work. No. That wasn't right. I *needed* to reunite with my family and *then* get back to work. So, in order to salvage my career, I had to do things their way.

The car door opened with a sharp click. The bright desert sun assaulted my eyes. Squinting, and shielding my face, I emerged slowly, weakly. An American soldier steadied me by supporting me under my elbow, eliciting a flurry of murmurs from the crowd. How bad did I look? In my mind, old-time cameras clicked and flashed, but nothing made any noise like that anymore, nor was a flash necessary in a region with the most insane sun on the planet.

My stomach turned as the soldier helped me up the stairs, his face awash with worry as I shakily took each step.

"Just take it one step at a time, sir," he whispered in a tone usually reserved for children.

Sure, I'd been starved and beaten for months, but my company's doctors assured me that I would suffer no lingering, long term *physical* issues. I forced my back straight and ascended the last three stairs quickly, barely stumbling over the last.

To seem stronger, I had demanded a podium even though they recommended I be seated. I always had an idea in my head about forced recovery, forced success. *My idea, right?* If I had no choice, then succeeding was my only option. *Surrender to your success.* Many people, including my wife Janna, had pointed out problems in my line of thinking, but I attributed it to many of my triumphs in my life. Something akin to necessity being the mother of invention, but in more of a backed into a corner situation.

I also requested an outdoor press conference. I'd been stuck in that dungeon so long, the idea of being in even a large room *answering questions again* gave me the shakes. Laura had the idea of having my statements given on the tarmac near my waiting plane. She said the visuals showing me coming home would speak volumes about hope and resolution. Her suggestion wasn't a bad idea.

Reaching the podium, my shaky legs challenged my forced success philosophy. I willed the bottom half of my body to remain steady as a rock and scanned the crowd for familiar faces. Nobody famous looked back. I supposed my predicament wasn't important enough for them to make the trip. No friends, either. Did I have any friends outside of work? With all the travel, projects, and family demands, I rarely made time for friends.

David? Dave, my neighbor, was a friend. Not a good enough friend to make the trip though. I didn't blame him, as I doubted I would travel as far as Kansas City for him, let alone the other side of the world. That was the old me. *I'm going to be a better friend to Dave.*

The scene hadn't played out like I imagined it would. I had dreamed that the entire world longed for my safe return, and that I would dominate the news cycle for months. Instead, the whole ordeal felt like the media, and my country, were just checking the boxes, reducing my months of trauma to an easily digestible sound bite. I frowned across the crowd that contained only a few mics and cameras. Most casually held out their phones for recording. The atmosphere and lacking excitement among the onlookers rivaled the desert for dryness.

I had a vision of my funeral. Take away the press, replace Laura with an intern, and that would cover it. Would Janna and Millie go to my funeral? *God. The fact that I wonder at all is reason enough to change.* I exhaled into the single microphone on the podium. The loud rumble quieted the murmurs in the crowd and brought every eye that wasn't already fixed on me, to me.

All resentment left me in a wave. If I died today, my funeral would be a pathetic reflection of my meaningless life. These strangers had come to see me, hear me, and celebrate my survival. Furthermore, they wanted to tell the world about me. They would tell my story to Janna and Millie, the story I couldn't tell them by phone over their sobs of joy and pain when I first called them. These strangers, these new allies of mine, wanted me to be okay and wanted to hear me say it. These new friends would help me start my new life

Husband to Janna. Father to Millie. But better this time.

I grinned. The gesture lifted the spirits of the entire crowd, bringing them in closer to the podium. Casually held phones were now held firm and high above their heads.

"Thank you for coming," I said hoarsely due to the arid desert air that bit at my throat. "I am thankful to be here and thankful to the millions of people who wished for my safe return." I gave the crowd a thumbs up. "Your thoughts and prayers worked perfectly."

The crowd responded with an appropriately sensible chuckle. Mr. Spencer stood still, statuelike, with no reaction. I eyed Laura near the bottom of the stairs. Her slight frown and miniscule head shake meant for me to stick to the script. Honestly, in the moment, I needed to cut her some slack as well. The company she represented provided financial security to nearly forty-thousand people, and the products of Bright Futures helped provide power to entire regions on this planet. Laura was on the side of the light and likely a good person to boot. I smiled at her and Mr. Spencer. He didn't react at all, beyond his perpetual smirk. Heck, I cut him some slack as well.

This was it. This was my time to start anew. I took a deep breath and let it out slowly enough to not bother the microphone. I raised my chin. "I won't keep you all long as I don't have a lot to say. I don't remember being taken, and I don't remember much of what happened. I was held in a dark room. I don't know where or by whom. I'm just glad to be free and cannot wait to be with my wife and daughter." I gestured toward Laura. "Laura tells me that some of you have questions."

The questions were pre-approved and came to me completely benign. What do you look forward to the most? *Outside of seeing my girls? Sleeping in my bed.* How is your health after such an ordeal? *I'm a little down, but definitely not out. I expect a full recovery.* Are you going straight back to Nebraska? *Of course. There's no place I'd rather be.* I answered all the small questions about my future and my family and if I'm a hero. *A hero? No, I don't think so. I'm just lucky to be alive.*

Laura began to climb the stairs, indicating the questions had come to an end. I nodded to her. My newfound reverence for the crowd that had gathered remained, but I had grown tired. It was time to board that plane, go to sleep, and finally go home.

"Do you know why you, specifically, were taken?" a man asked with an accent, a French accent. *Swiss French? How would I know that? Did I know someone from there?*

Laura's eyes shot daggers at the man before I even registered that the man had directed the question to me. Weren't we finished? I turned to the man.

"Money," I said.

Tilting her head toward the reporter, Laura rushed toward me.

The man wore brown pants, a bit on the worn side, and a blue, collared, button up shirt with the sleeves rolled up. Unlike Laura, all of his clothes were wrinkled. His dark hair, peppered with gray, rested shoulder length in random curls. He peered at me through thick-lensed glasses.

"With the chaos that ensued during your rescue, have you been given any more details than . . . money?"

Chaos? Rescue?

Scrambling to the podium, Laura fumbled toward the microphone. "Details of Gideon's release are still unfolding. We do not know any more than you do." Laura looped her arm around mine. "It's been a long day for Gideon. Thank you all for coming to see him, but at this time there will be no further questions."

Laura led me toward the stairs. I glanced at the reporter who asked the questions. He scribbled in a journal, not looking up at me. So, they were keeping details from me? *That won't help my new attitude.*

Revival.

"Whenever you are ready, sir," My driver, Andy, said.

I made it home, but I struggled to remember the events that brought me to this point, just like my captivity. The plane ride home, getting in this car, I may as well have watched it in a movie. The experience resembled sleepwalking, as I didn't feel in control, but concentrating on the events brought every moment to my mind. Consciously unconscious, maybe. The therapist had told me that I could be blocking memories like a child does trauma, but these memories were not blocked, the smallest focus brought them back to me.

My company had spared no expense with my transportation. Constant premium cars with drivers and especially the private jets were luxuries I could get used to, but that wasn't why I didn't leave the car. I couldn't breathe and my heart raced. My reason for life, my mantra, Janna and Millie, waited inside that house, but I couldn't budge. Frozen with fear, I didn't dare move even though it should have been the easiest thing to do in my life.

"We're early," I said. "They won't be expecting me, yet." I could have texted or called, but I didn't and now it was too late.

Janna. I knew her better than I knew myself. Or, at least I believed that once. Things had been different since I left for the Middle East. Our marriage had suffered for years before then. I couldn't imagine what she'd gone through when I was held captive. And Millie. I refused to even think about how she felt for fear that my heart would tear itself apart.

I can force this, can't I? Ugh.

I closed my eyes and leaned back in my seat. Breathing deeply, I focused on what I wanted. *Get in there.* I wanted a new start with them. I couldn't start over if I didn't start at all. *I need a new life.* I had to be a better husband, a better father. *Fine. No choice. Go in.*

"Thanks for the ride, Andy," I said.

Andy made eye contact in the rear-view mirror and nodded. "Have a nice evening, sir."

I exited the vehicle and looked over my house and the yard. The sun had started its descent in the early autumn Nebraska sky, casting shadows across my front lawn. I'd lived here for fifteen years, but the house seemed unfamiliar, like I was seeing it for the first time, having only seen it in pictures before, pictures in the mind of the man I was before. Was it a good thing or bad thing that my entire life from before seemed to belong to someone else?

This house, though . . .. Compared to where I'd stayed the last six months, my house had more in common with the Palace of Versailles. I glanced over my shoulder as Andy's car rolled away down my cobblestone driveway, shrouded in large, picturesque oak trees which clung to their red, yellow, and brown leaves in a futile effort to stave off winter. The driveway *was* a tad on the opulent side as was the rest of my house.

The front of the all brick house had pillars meant to pay homage to Greek architecture. We had five bedrooms and seven bathrooms for three people. We had our own entertainment floor with magnificent areas dedicated to watching movies, fitness, a bar and a separate recreational area with ping pong, foosball, and a few of my favorite arcade games from my childhood.

We all made good money at Bright Futures and had little to spend it on in Nebraska, so we all bought these million-dollar homes, we all played golf at the country club, and we all had ridiculously nice cars. Our extravagances were outrageous in retrospect, but nothing on the level of having my own private jet, like the one that flew me home. I always thought I would make it to that level, but now all the baubles and improvidences seemed pointless. I didn't need more stuff. The people in my life held the only true value to me.

The house had been kept up well in my absence, perfectly to be more accurate. Janna hadn't let anything go and had even seen to replacing the shutters that had taken a beating during a particularly rough snowstorm two winters past. I'd taken a beating over the last six months; would Janna replace me? I hoped she'd had help and hadn't fixed them herself. Janna always wanted to do things herself. Replacing the shutters had likely been on my to-do list, so I needed to remember to tell her that I noticed and that they looked great.

I arrived at the front door and reached for the knob but hesitated. Should I ring, should I knock or call before entering? I'd never been obligated to do so before, but everything was different now. *A stranger in my own home.* I looked away from the door, down the row of bushes. A metal sign leaned against the house, blocked so that I couldn't see it from the street. I squeezed between the hedges to get a better look at it—a real estate sign with "For Sale" in bold letters on top.

She really was going to leave me. Or had she thought me dead and decided to move on? I sighed. Would she have sold the house without me? *It doesn't matter. This is a new start.*

I wriggled back to the front door and rang the doorbell. No noise came from within, indicating that no one was home. Were they home? *I should have called.* Then, a shout and a scuffle of feet rushed toward the door. It flung open revealing Janna and Millie, tears in their eyes.

Millie leapt for me, grabbing me around my neck.

My eyes welled as I embraced her. "Millie. I missed you so much."

She released me and wiped her eyes. "I can't believe you're back." She smiled so big that my heart ached.

"You're earlier than you said," Janna said with a happy, jovial tone.

How I longed for her to be happy.

"I know," I replied, giddy with excitement. "That's the problem when you fly privately. They always get you there too early." I laughed and they humored my small joke.

Moving farther inside, I closed the door behind me.

Janna's light blue eyes sparkled, probably watery from the tearful reunion that had already gone so much better than I'd dared to hope. Purposely tousled dark brown hair flowed to her shoulders in the way a model or movie star would wear. She had mastered the ability to look nonchalant with her style, but always managed to seem extremely put together, even though she said she didn't spend any time on it. Like the house, it was as if Janna and I had just met for the first time.

The almost invisible patch of freckles across her adorable, slightly upturned nose brought a reality to the face I had only dreamt about every night since I had been taken. Her radiance filled me with comfort. *I'm home.*

"You look amazing," I told her, opening my arms slightly, but not moving toward her.

She embraced me, softly at first, then tightly. I reciprocated. Her body jerked when she fought back tears, then she coughed sadly and let her sobs come. She cried on my shoulder while Millie embraced the two of us.

Janna put her hands on my waist and pushed away. "You've lost a *lot* of weight." She grinned.

"My diet and exercise routine aren't for everyone." I held my hands out, admiring my frail physique. "But you can't argue with the results."

Millie laughed. "You can borrow some of my clothes, dad."

"Millie!" Janna lightly swatted our daughter's arm.

"He knows I'm kidding."

"It's fine." It really was, and I was happy to be joking with Millie already. "I'm not looking like myself, but I don't think I'll ever go back to the way I was before. It wasn't healthy."

"Oh really?" Janna asked, probably rhetorically, possibly mocking.

I looked down, avoiding eye contact with either of them. "I don't want to do much of anything like I did before."

"I'm glad you're back, Dad," Millie said like a ray of sunshine, filling me with more hope.

"I'm hungry all of a sudden." The words escaped my lips before I completely realized their truth. I had been eating sporadically since waking from my nightmare, but I had never been hungry. Being around them healed me, made me truly want to *be* alive, not just say it in my head.

"I'll make you something," Janna said, grabbing me by the forearm. "Or we can go out. What sounds good?"

My eyes teared up at the sentiment and mood in the room. Earlier it seemed impossible that it could go this well. If I wanted, everything would go back to the way it was, like we never missed a beat. But I didn't want normal. I wanted better.

"No, I'll cook." I slid my arm through Janna's and gripped her hand gently. "I'll grill and it'll be fun. I think it will be good for me to be active instead of sitting around."

"Aren't you tired, honey?" Janna squeezed my fingers. "Why not let me get you a drink and something to eat. You need rest."

"No." I grabbed Millie's hand, holding both of theirs up. "No, I'm not tired. I want to spend time with you. I want to make up for lost time, more than just the last six months. I also want to be a better friend, a better neighbor, a better person."

Janna shrugged then let go of me. "Okay Gideon." She smiled with only half of her mouth. It was cute. Had I ever noticed that before?

Living.

"You better turn those," Dave said from over my shoulder.

I stopped staring at Millie and Janna talking, laughing and setting the outside table together and lazily glanced down at the small fires on my grill where only steaks should have been. Jerking my hand, first for the steaks, I then scrambled to find something to turn the meat with.

"Here you go, buddy." Dave held out my tongs and smiled.

"Thanks," I said, snatching them from his hand. Our back lawns touched, so he and Anne must have just come through the yards. Not surprising, we shared that level of comfort with them.

The weather bordered on the chilly side, but Dave wasn't ready to admit defeat to winter. He wore red plaid shorts, a blue polo shirt, and flip flops. I wore old jeans, held up by a belt because of my weight loss, and a short sleeve t-shirt, but I should have had on a jacket in this weather. I hated being cold, but for some reason, I wasn't. Why wasn't I cold?

Dave huffed out a laugh. "Your steaks."

I turned around and flipped the steaks, poked at the foil-wrapped potatoes and shook the basket holding the mixed vegetables. Everything seemed about ready. *Nice job . . . Gideon. Husband to Janna. Father to . . . .*

Turning back to Dave, I tilted my head toward Janna and Millie. "Sorry. I just missed them so much that it's hard to focus on anything else."

Without warning, Dave swarmed over me, locking me in a tight bear hug. "It's great to have you back." His tone seemed . . . filled with genuine sentiment. His voice cracked a little.

I awkwardly patted his back, while still holding my tongs. "Thanks man. It's great to be back."

Sniffing as he pulled away, he squeezed both my shoulders and looked me in the eyes. Much younger than Janna and me, Dave resembled a *GQ* cover model. Thick, almost black hair, a perfect, square jawline, and envy-inducing long lashes would make a lesser man jealous. *Okay, I'm jealous.*

I grinned at him, but he turned away.

"Anne, did you grab it? I forgot," Dave yelled, but not in a mean way.

Anne was at least twice my daughter's age, which made her just age appropriate for my twenty-eight-year-old neighbor. Straight long blonde hair draped her golden-ratioed face. Her trendy, long-sleeved turtle-neck dress gave off both leisure and chic vibes, while also being cut in a way to let everyone know that she spent hours at the gym. Anne was very attractive, but never someone that I thought of as a partner. I'd really only had eyes for Janna. In that way, I'd always been a good husband. At least I had that part right.

David placed his hand on Anne's waist, eliciting a wry smile from her. Love is love, and by the way these two couldn't keep their hands off each other, they were very much in the "love is a verb" camp. Honestly though, what else did they have to do? Dave and Anne had made their money investing Anne's inheritance and rarely had to work.

Anne strolled toward me carrying a six-pack of beer in her hands.

I raised my brows, then scrunched my nose, watching Anne come closer.

She pinched her lips, looking very much like the cat that ate the canary. "It's that IPA you love from the west coast." She shot a glance at Dave. "Dave said this was the one."

I studied the beer, but I didn't recognize it. The label said, "Sulating." She had to be right. These were my only friends outside of work. I looked at Dave who worked on a frown. I glanced over my shoulder as Janna and Millie joined us and exchanged greetings with our neighbors.

I jerked my head back to Anne. *Don't be rude,* but how could I not remember my favorite beer? I needed to see someone about these lapses. *Not another shrink, though.* "That *is* my favorite. How'd you find it?"

Anne let out a breath that I didn't know she was holding. "Dave found it. He went all the way to Omaha." She smiled and handed me the six-pack, which I graciously accepted.

Dave nodded at the beer, imploring me to drink one.

Janna had engaged Anne in compliments about her sweater-dress. Millie fiddled with the grill, turning the heat down to the lowest setting. My daughter grabbed the tongs out of my hand and started turning the steaks again.

I presented the six-pack to Dave. "Do you want one?"

Dave said thanks and pulled one out for each of us. He grabbed his keys out of his pocket, popped the caps, and handed me mine. "Cheers," he said.

We tapped bottle tips, and I sipped a small drink. The bitterness overwhelmed me. My throat closed off, protecting me from the disgusting liquid. I coughed uncontrollably, bent over, and spit Sulating everywhere. My nose burned; my eyes flooded.

More than one hand pounded my back while a chorus of inquiries about my health accompanied my struggle.

"Is it cold enough?" Dave asked. "Dammit. I picked it up today. I thought it was cold enough."

"It's fine." I coughed again and straightened. "It's good. It just went down the wrong pipe."

A sea of wide eyes and tight lips greeted me. How could they not be worried? With my frail physique and inability to do something I'd done a million times, like drink a beer, I had to be a sad picture. I quickly sipped from my *favorite* beer, again, and this time willed it down without incident, even though my throat fought all the way to my stomach. "See." I grimaced, betraying my words. "All good."

"It's all right, man." Dave patted my back. "You're gonna need a minute to get back on your fee—"

"I'm fine," I said sharply. Dave reeled back. I shouldn't have done that. I grabbed his arm and relaxed my face. In a congenial tone, I said, "I am fine. Sorry."

"Don't worry about it. We're all here for you." Dave jerked his head toward the grill. "But, we should probably go and let you eat those steaks. They smell awesome."

"You should stay and eat with us," I said.

Dave and Anne protested, but Janna and Millie told them they only wanted half a steak anyway. My neighbors said that half a steak was plenty for them as well. The friendly group excitably negotiated portioning the rest of the food, after which sent everyone into a frenzy to put the table together for dinner. I had trouble finding a place to help as they all leapt into action. Millie and Dave pulled the food from the grill, placing it all on plates and bowls that Anne and Janna had magically summoned. Before I knew it, we all stood around the patio table, David and Millie setting two pitchers of water at either end. Their speed would have been admirable if it wasn't due to them trying to stay busy and not address the weak elephant in the room. Except, I wasn't large like an elephant, and we were outside, but that goes without saying. And *had* they moved quickly, or was I stuck in a similar daze that I'd suspected accompanied the missing details of my last six months? I could recall *these* details as they happened, though.

"That was fast," I said, clasping my hands together.

"We've been eating a lot of meals together, lately" Millie said. She looked away, licking her lips.

Because of the shared trauma? I get it.

"That warms my heart," I said, smiling at each of them in turn. Dave smiled back enthusiastically, Ann's flat lips and nod seemed apprehensive, Millie grinned fully, and Janna . . .. She didn't meet my eyes, but hers were watery and focused on her plate. Maybe I weirded them out with my silent smiles. *Better say something else.* "I hope that's a tradition that continues." I raised my beer to the neighbors. "Thank you, Anne and David for being good friends to me, even in my absence."

Dave raised his beer, quickly glancing at Janna, then back to me. The rest of the table raised their waters.

"I'm just over-the-moon happy to be home." My voice cracked.

My family and friends reflected my sentiment. Raising the beer bottle to my lips, I only tasted it, didn't take a drink. Did my commitment to being a better person cause a physical aversion to alcohol? I tilted my head, pondering that possibility.

Dinner conversation eventually settled on details of my capture. Their questions were short, not probing, and easier than the questions the reporters had given me. These people were important to me, the most important, so I had to be open with them. If not them, then who?

"It wasn't easy," I said. My heart raced. Could I tell them how weak, how helpless I was? I had to, but I couldn't find the courage to look at them. I pushed around my steak that I had barely touched. A few bites into it filled me quickly. "It wasn't easy. Hah." I mocked my earlier words. "You can't repeat anything I say, though."

I paused but didn't wait for a reply. David may have said that he would be quiet. I looked at Millie, her eyes teared up. What would a twelve-year-old think of her dad? I had to tell her. I had to tell all of them. "I was beaten and tortured over there."

Anne gasped, more of a shriek. The rest of the table quieted, Janna covering her quivering chin. I couldn't look back at Millie. *I am a coward. No, force yourself through this. Father to Millie.* I raised my eyes to my daughter who sat stoically; a tear rolled down her face. "I'll tell you all again that I'm fine. I don't look it, and I don't act like I'm fine, but I'm actually better than ever. Going through this . . . thing . . . has made me realize what's important." I scanned the table full of sympathetic faces. "It's also made me aware what a jerk I've been to the most important people in my life."

"Never," David protested.

I chuckled. "Maybe. Maybe not, but that won't stop me from being better." I looked at Janna. She grinned, cutely again with half her mouth.

"Why did they do it?" David asked.

"David," Anne said admonishingly.

"What?" David shrugged.

"It's okay." I held up my hand, to reassure them. "I want you all to know everything. They wanted to know how to release the uranium fuel, the dangerous stuff, probably to make a bomb. Even though most of it's low enriched, things would get messy if they got their hands on it."

"You didn't tell them how, did you?" David asked hurriedly.

"David!" Anne rose from her seat.

"Haha." I lifted both hands up in front of me. Anne sat back down. "It's okay. No, David, I didn't." I shook my head. "I couldn't. My system is designed too well. I told them it was impossible every time they asked."

"I bet they didn't like that answer." David's words trailed off, and he looked down at his lap, shaking his head and avoiding Anne's wide-eyed glare. "I can hear it now. I'll shut up."

"They did *not* like that answer, but it was the only answer." *Facts are facts. Truth, for that matter, is the truth.* I looked toward the nearby woods, thinking of security keys, peer review, double biometric secondary factors, rapid oxidation, and the intricate physical housings with key-like couplers—and worked out at least three viable ways to bypass every bit of it.

Safety.

After Anne and David left, we relaxed in the downstairs entertainment room. Janna lounged nearby, reading a book, and I lost my ninth match of foosball in a row to Millie but not by as many points this time.

"I don't remember you being this bad," Millie said.

"Maybe you're just that much better," I said.

Millie shook her head. "Are you letting me win? You never did before."

Looking up from her book, Janna eyed us worriedly, then sipped at her glass of red wine.

"No. I'm not letting you win, and you won't win the next one." I grinned to counter my daughter's smirk. "But I am getting older and slower while you keep getting faster and faster. It's probably just your reflexes."

"Okay," Millie said doubtfully. "I'll beat you one more time, then I want to go up to bed and read."

I rolled the ball through the hole in the side. Almost instantly, Millie jerked her wrist, launching a shot at my goal. Luckily, it bounced off my player without scoring. I seized two of my handles, controlling two rows of players. Tapping the ball lightly, I set up my forward row for a quick shot, seized on it and scored. I looked up to Millie in amazement.

"Nice shot," she shouted.

Janna grinned our way. I closed my eyes and took a breath. Everything that I'd hoped for while being held captive seemed to be unfolding before me.

Crack. Pop.

I opened my eyes as the ball dropped into my goal box.

"One to one," Millie said with a giggle. "You need to pay attention."

"All right. All right." I shook my head. "No mercy."

We played without banter and with more intensity than previous matches, trading scores back and forth. In the end, Millie won again, but only by one point.

"Good game. I thought I had you." I futilely twirled a couple of rows of tiny soccer players.

"Me too." Millie's smile morphed into a yawn. "Bleh. I guess I'm tired and probably won't read much now."

"What book are you reading?"

"I finished *The Hobbit* and I'm about half through *Fellowship*."

"Good job. That's pretty tough reading for an eleven-year-old."

Millie scrunched her brows. "It would be, but I'm twelve, Dad."

Millie. Birthday, June 25th. She had turned twelve while I was gone. While I pondered that, Millie walked around the table and gave me a tight hug, not saying anything.

I embraced her, fighting tears of joy. *I'm home.*

She pushed away and smiled again; a twinkle of a revelation caught her eyes. "I guess I'll get to see you again tomorrow, Dad."

"Of course. I'll make pancakes."

She giggled and headed for the stairs. "Okay." Millie shook her head.

Pancakes. Do I make pancakes? Why did I say pancakes?

"Did you let her win?" Janna asked.

"No." I rubbed my forehead. "I guess I was better before. I'm struggling with the weirdest things."

"Like memory?" Janna set her book down, stood up, and moved close to me.

I grabbed her hand. She didn't pull away. "Laura had me see a shrink, but I think I need to find someone else to talk to."

"What's my mother's name?" Janna asked, tilting her head.

"Dolores."

"Hmmm."

I winced, but why? I said the correct name.

"What's my sign?"

"Aquarius." My face flushed. *Is being questioned triggering me?*

Janna grabbed my other hand and smiled her half-smile. "It seems to me like you remember the important things." She pulled me close, wrapping my hands around her back.

I froze within her arms, daring not to breathe or move lest I do something to make her pull away. "I noticed the shutters."

"What shutters?" Janna asked softly.

"I noticed you fixed the shutters outside. I'd never had them repaired, but you got it done. They look great." I didn't mention the for-sale sign.

"Oh." Janna pulled against me tighter, then yawned against my chest. "Let's go to bed."

"Together?" I asked.

The week before I left for my trip, I'd slept in the guest room down here. I mentally crossed my fingers.

Janna didn't say anything, only turned and headed for the stairs, still holding one of my hands.

Following in silence, I focused on my footing and kept pace with Janna. *Don't stumble. Don't pull back.* For some odd reason, apprehensive feelings gnawed at my gut, like I didn't deserve any of this, like I couldn't just pick up as if the *jerk* that lived here before didn't exist, like I wasn't being genuine, like I was a fraud.

I followed her into our bedroom.

She spun around and kissed me.

My doubts fled in an instant.

* * *

Staring at the ceiling, I marveled at how quickly I had gotten my life back on track. It didn't matter if I deserved any of it; I wouldn't take it for granted this time. Furthermore, I would do everything in my power to earn this love.

Janna's arm, her thigh, and the moonlight were all that touched my skin. There wasn't a place on Earth I'd rather be.

I breathed deeply. A click echoed through my expansive house. In the nighttime silence, the house made all kinds of noises, a crick here, a groan there, a whistle with the wind, but that had been the first click. That one click, unnoticeable during the day, roared like a gong in the still of the night.

I scrambled through an inventory of the sounds that I'd never noticed before, but no clicks. An uneasy feeling swept over me. Something was off.

A board creaked, but quickly, unnaturally, silenced. *We aren't alone.*

"Janna," I whispered, shaking her awake.

She moaned in response.

"Someone's in the house," I whispered quickly and sprang from bed, jumping into my jeans.

"Don't go out there," Janna said, not lowering her voice. "I'll call the police."

"Millie's *out there*," I said back.

Janna nodded and picked up her phone. She lowered her voice when talking to the police.

Every shadow in the hallway loomed like an intruder. Cold sweat chilled me, and hurried breaths reluctantly followed me into the family room where the moonlight traced the unmistakable outline of a very *real*, large person standing by my open patio door. Why hadn't the alarm tripped?

Did I know him? He seemed familiar. "Dave." My voice unfortunately cracked as I said my neighbor's name, but the man didn't answer. I stood straighter, confident, in spite of the silhouette that seemed to grow larger. Surely, they had seen me enter the room, even with the twenty feet between us. "We've called the police. You need to go."

The shadow at the door folded its arms but did not budge.

Mouthing words that didn't come out, I gaped, astonished that someone would have the audacity not only to break into my home, but to just stand there when the police were on the way. What kind of person would do that? *A dangerous one.*

A feeling—a warning—sent a chill down my spine. Reflexively, I ducked and rolled over my shoulder, barely avoiding a rounding foot that came from behind. I crouched and spun about, facing my new attacker.

Another kick, more direct than the first, rushed towards my abdomen.

I *caught* the boot with both hands. Gripping it tightly, I pushed back and twisted, forcing the person down to one knee. *She* grunted, then laughed. "Idti." Small frame, fit and agile. *Anne?*

Glancing over my shoulder, I looked for the first intruder. He had disappeared.

A kick to my groin sent me to my knees. I lifted my chin in time to catch a blurred glimpse of another blow, this time across my jaw, dropping me limply to the floor.

Quick steps retreated outside while shuffling steps advanced from the hallway. I groaned and tried to simultaneously apply comfort to my jaw and groin. *That better not have been Anne; barbecues will get weird.* My aloofness unnerved me more than the confrontation.

The lights flashed on, blinding me.

Janna hurried to my side and scooped her arms around me, helping me up, coming to my rescue.

"They're gone. The police are on their way." Janna looked worriedly toward the door and down the hallway leading to our daughter's room. "Millie." She *dropped* me onto the floor, but I had regained enough strength to hold myself up. I chased after in time to witness Janna barrel through the door to Millie's room and flip on the lights.

Millie sat up out of bed. "What the—"

What the *what*? Did Millie curse around her friends? *Weird thing to be focusing on.* I sat on the bed next to Janna, placing a hand on her back while she cried, explained, and prodded Millie, ensuring our daughter was okay. The intruders hadn't bothered her.

"I'll figure out what's up with the alarm tomorrow," I said, glancing toward Millie's open door. The sound of sirens grew louder outside. "For now, let's get some regular clothes on. The police are here."

Senseless.

I dried off the last plate and set it on the counter. Pancakes turned out pretty easy to make, and as an added bonus, they were delicious. Millie said so.

Janna clanked open the stepladder by the patio door. "We're probably not in danger in the short-term, but I need to know why the alarm didn't go off." Janna sipped her coffee, then set it on the top step.

I grabbed my mug and ambled over to offer my two cents. *I'm the engineer here.* I peered out the patio door at the off-duty police officer's car, lurking a way down the driveway, the early morning light barely clipping the top of his sedan. The rest of the vehicle remained shrouded in darkness, like the interior.

"Yeah, not in any danger." I gently rubbed the small bruise on my chin, then sipped my coffee and focused on Janna.

"You don't think he'll keep us safe?" Janna asked.

I didn't answer, but no, I didn't think one off-duty police officer made us completely safe.

Janna tugged at something on the top door sensor that looked like a gum wrapper. "That shouldn't have worked," she mumbled. She pulled the silver wrapping off with some difficulty, like it had been *stuck* to the sensor.

"Ah," she exclaimed, placing the small piece of metal back on the sensor, then pulling it off again. "This little thing is magnetized. Our security system must be pretty primitive."

"I'm off to the bus stop," Millie yelled heading for the front door.

"No." I shook my head. "I'm taking you, but I still don't think you should go."

"We're taking you," Janna corrected. "And this is how we deal with things now."

Millie cinched her backpack tighter and stood straighter. "By moving forward."

I smiled, sheepishly. Of course, Janna and Millie had been through a lot, all my fault. Their ordeal changed them, and they came out stronger. This lone incident wouldn't break them.

Janna lifted her chin, resolutely, but she didn't need to convince me. I couldn't come in and change everything just because I'd domineered before. No longer. I needed to do everything better.

I locked the patio door and led the way to the garage. Hesitantly, I creaked the door open, not sure what would be waiting for me. My hand hurt from gripping the doorknob too tightly.

I flipped on the lights, revealing our three electric vehicles, all luxury models because that used to be important to me. The sedan, the SUV, and the hard-to-get sportscar—how cliche for a Midwestern suburban man plagued with the burden of having too much money.

Janna walked past me holding up a key fob and heading for the SUV. "I'll drive."

Oh yeah, I would have needed that. Where do we keep those? I glanced over my shoulder and flinched at Millie.

She tapped on her phone, opening the garage doors. *Clever girl.* At least they understood how everything worked.

We didn't say anything as Janna drove out of the garage and down the driveway, past the saluting officer we had hired. The stress from my kidnapping with the added trauma from the break-in must have had us all in various states of shock. Even my burgeoning joy from being with Janna and Millie couldn't keep my mind from drifting to the break-in.

"Did they take anything?" Millie asked.

I opened my mouth to say, "No," but Janna's sigh stopped me.

"Only one thing that I know of." Janna kept her focus on the road.

What? She hadn't said anything to me.

"They took the ceramic turtle bowl you made me at school two years ago."

The bowl had been on Janna's vanity in our bathroom. She kept some earrings and bracelets in it. My eyes popped. That meant one of the burglars had crossed through our bedroom, while we were *distracted.*

"Did they take your jewelry?" Millie asked, her voice strained.

"No." Janna huffed. "It doesn't make any sense. They dumped out my jewelry and just took the bowl. I searched the house. Everything else seems to be there."

Why would they take something like that? I tried to steal a glance from Janna, but her attention remained focused on driving. She likely puzzled out that at least one of them had been in our room. How did that make her feel? Upgrading our security needed to be addressed quickly.

"Are you sure that it didn't get knocked under something?" I asked. "Your vanity can get pretty messy." I winced after saying that. I didn't mean to shame her or anything like that, but it *did* get messy.

"No, I'm sure." She slapped my arm, playfully. "And my vanity is organized. There's just a lot on it."

"Since you guys are driving me, we have time to get coffee," Millie said with a tinge of hope.

I shrugged. When did her school start? *Millie has to be at school by eight-twenty.* I looked at my watch which read seven thirty-eight. I twisted around to the back seat. "We just had coffee. Do you drink coffee now?"

"I like-a-latte." Millie strung the sounds together making a play on the words.

"Do we have time?" I asked Janna, but the calculations ran through my head in parallel. The coffee joint we frequented was only about three minutes away. Even with a line, we would be in and out in less than twenty minutes. Millie would still be early for school.

"New Moon?" Janna asked, glancing at the rearview mirror.

"Yeah," Millie answered.

"What's New Moon?" I asked.

"New Moon is a *newish* coffee shop. We love it," Millie said.

Great. Now I had no idea if we had enough time. For some reason, my stomach roiled at the idea of Millie being late for school. Why would that even matter? She could have taken the day off, and nobody would have blinked an eye with everything that had happened . . . that *kept* happening in Millie's life.

The trip to the coffee shop proved to be therapeutic. Millie talked about her writing project and a math test she planned on acing. Janna teased her about a boy, Alex Lehman. *Alex Lehman. Noted.* We laughed and joked and acted like everything was normal, comfortable, but every word of mine still echoed in my mind as if it came from someone else's mouth. *How long before I'm comfortable in my own skin again?*

New Moon Coffee took a page from every popular American coffee chain by decorating its walls, tables, and chairs in tans and dark browns to make customers think of and crave coffee. The white, faux marble countertops and stainless steel equipment behind them assured patrons that every effort had been taken to deliver a clean beverage. Millie ordered her latte, and I ordered— *Janna likes her coffee black, no room for creamer*—two medium black coffees.

"Michael, surprised to see you here," Janna said in a sarcastic tone behind me.

"Janna," the man said, oddly, like her simple name was difficult to pronounce.

I jerked my head around. *Michael. I don't know him, do I? I know him.* Michael wore a tweed sports jacket, jeans, a white button up shirt, and glasses, standard professor garb complete with elbow patches on the jacket. The man at least attempted to groom his mostly gray hair and beard, but stray tufts told me that he didn't much care about his appearance. *I don't know him.*

"Yes. We often joke that I practically live here." Michael laughed, his response in a thick Russian accent. *Definitely Russian, from somewhere far south like Sochi. Why did I know that when I couldn't remember where my key fobs were?*

Janna smiled at Michael and gestured to me. "This is my husband, Gideon."

"It is wonderful to have you . . . home." Michael held out a hand that I shook.

Russian. Sochi. The hair on the back of my neck stood on end. "Are you new to town?"

"No. Not new." He looked at Janna.

"Michael is a regular here, since New Moon opened."

"When was that?"

"Six months. Da."

A pain pierced the center of my head; dizziness overwhelmed me. I must have stumbled because Michael steadied me with a hand on my arm.

"Are you okay, Gideon?" Michael asked.

Flashes of recollection, like dreams and words mixing together, popped into my head. "I know someone like you. I know a Russian. Do I know you?"

"Gideon," Janna said in a hushed, reprimanding tone.

"All is right, Janna Mossert. Steady, my new friend Gideon. I know you have been through much, but we have never met, and I am not Russian." Michael flattened his lips.

I huffed a single laugh, eliciting wide eyes from Janna. "Not Russian?" I asked. This information existed in my brain. If his accent did not originate from the city of Sochi or nearby Adler, then I was a . . . I was a . . .. My legs turned to jelly.

Michael grabbed me under the arms with strong hands and poured me into the chair he had been sitting in. His grip, his quick actions, his posture and balance all indicated a military man and conflicted with his college professor's exterior.

I looked into his eyes, and they looked back, inquisitive, studious, diagnostic. Suddenly I was certain that this man worked as a doctor. My mind darted in every direction. First, I'd assumed him a professor, then a soldier, and lastly a doctor. A sharp pain pierced my skull. *Yes. Russian. Sochi. Doctor. Ogon.* My stomach twisted, the blood drained from my face, and I slumped in my chair.

"Gideon," Janna shrieked, this time with concern. "Let's get you home."

"No, let's get you to a hospital," Millie said, suddenly by my side. In fact, everyone in the coffee house now stared at my plight.

I nodded in defeat.

My brain hurt but more from a struggle for understanding than the sharp pain I'd briefly experienced. My wife and Millie, possibly just the two of them, ushered me to our car.

Janna and Millie slammed their car doors shut almost in unison, snapping me out of the miniature trance I'd succumbed to.

"Do you want to go to the hospital?" Janna asked, placing her hand on my forearm.

My gaze darted to her touch. "You don't think it's odd that a Russian man showed up right when I disappeared?"

"Honey," Janna patronized me. "You weren't in Russia."

My words repeated in my mind. I shook my head in disbelief, doubting myself as I jumped to ridiculous conclusions. Janna was right. My abductors were from the Middle East, not Russia. I pinched my forehead and couldn't summon a memory of any Russians that I knew personally. "You're right. I'm sorry." I met her worried look. "I'm fine. Let's get Millie to school."

I looked back at Millie, her wet eyes on the verge of tears. How could I keep doing this to them?

She held up a tray that held three beverages. "Coffee?"

I chuckled. "Yeah, Millie, thanks." I grabbed mine and Janna's and placed them in the front cup holders.

Russian. Sochi. Doctor.

"Ogon," I mumbled.

"What?" Janna asked.

"Nothing. I'm fine." *Ogon.*

Better.

Millie left the car for school with her head down, until a friend—
Dakota Lambert, from the nearby subdivision Cherry Court—lifted
her head, and hopefully her spirits.

"I'm going to make it up to her," I said.

"I know you will." Janna gripped my hand tightly. "Do you want
to go home and rest?"

Shaking my head, I glanced at Janna. Her wide eyes studied
me. She still worried.

"I'd like to go into the office and talk to them about upgrading
our home security system," I said.

Janna tilted her head.

"When do you go to work?" I asked.

Raising her wrist in front of her face, Janna read her watch. "I
teach a class at nine, but I need to be there around eight-thirty, so
now, to set up."

"I'll go with you, and help you get ready. Then we can go to my
work after your class."

"What will you do during my class?"

"I'll take it."

Janna spat out a laugh, then covered her mouth. "Sorry. I
mean. It's just that you've never shown any interest in my studio
before." She shook her head and pulled away. "Also, it's not a
beginner class. Just drop me off and head into the office."

"No." I lifted my chin. "I'm interested in your class. Pilates,
right?"

She nodded and smiled her half-smile.

"It's three days a week. I can commit to that." *I could.*

Janna sniffed and wiped at the corner of her eye.

"What?" I asked. "I'm wearing sweatpants."

"Ha ha." She snorted. "This will be good—if you can keep up.
Focus on your core and find your true center. I think it will help
you clear your mind." She pointed a finger at my head. "And your
head is kind'a a mess right now." Her face paled. "Sorry."

Placing a hand on Janna's shoulder, I gently squeezed before
speaking. "No, you're right. Exercise can help me work through
some of this"—I rubbed my face with my other hand—"whatever
this is."

Janna pulled away from the school parking lot. I marveled at
her brightened face and wry smile. She knew more than anybody
what was in store for me and how much I would suffer through the
class and after. Even with the looming threat of pain and possible

indignities, the theory that exercise would do me good tracked well. I had to do something to fix my head.

The trip to the studio didn't take long, its location not at all far from the school or the house or my office. Having everything close by brought many people to small communities like this, the benefits and comforts not lost on us when we moved here, but every passing year threatened to destroy this convenience as more and more people moved to our smallish Nebraska town, stretching the border farther and farther into the countryside. New Moon Coffee wasn't the only new business to invade Cascade Valley during my absence.

Tel Aviv or Berlin would welcome a building as modern as Janna's studio. Double A-frames connected by a suspended bridge-like floor, with facing exterior windows that extended from floor to ceiling, allowed visibility from the street into five separate work areas, two of which were already active with classes. Since a child, Janna had dreamed of owning her own fitness business, and Powerhouse Studio embodied that dream.

After exiting the car, I stepped briskly toward the building, then slowed and stared at the asphalt in the parking lot. This represented *her* dream, and *I* hadn't been there for her. She did this, not me. Shame welled up inside of me. I bit my bottom lip. Old Gideon's words hissed in my mind. *This business will fail before five years are up.* I had told her that five years ago. I didn't truly believe that, did I?

Janna walked up behind me and pinched me on both sides of my waist. "Having second thoughts?"

"No." I glanced over my shoulder and grinned at her. *I need to be better than the old Gideon.* "I'm so proud of you. You really did it."

Her head jerked back, then she smiled, although quickly covered it up. "Thank you." Her tone questioned more than stated. Janna tilted her head, beckoning me into her studio. Surely, I'd been inside before. Nobody could be that heartless. Still, nothing looked familiar, and the experience certainly seemed like a new one.

Jessica—*Jessica Michaels, thirty-four, married to Geoff, two daughters, worked here since the studio opened*—greeted us at the door holding a digital tablet and ran straight into an update for Janna, including an instructor's cancellation which particularly irked both of the women. Jessica volunteered to cover for the absenteed instructor. Was Jessica a good person, a good friend to Janna?

I squinted at Jessica. Her short, narrow chin and almost invisible lips contrasted with her oversized eyes. Handsome, but not striking features, made it difficult to remember if I knew her or not.

She raised her eyebrows at me. "Gideon. It's so nice to see you."

She seems sincere. Her expectant, possibly wanting eyes awaited some type of response. *Good to see you, too? Thank you? Should I hug her? Am I a hugger now?* I opened my arms slightly, then retreated. "Likewise." I settled on a smile.

Jessica's short laugh felt a little haughty, but that really just seemed like the way she talked. She turned her attention back to Janna and scrunched her brows.

"Gideon is taking my class today." Janna folded her arms.

The woman's mouth started and stopped in an attempt at speaking while Janna and I glanced at each other.

Janna laughed. "He'll be fine. We'll keep him in the back."

Class was held in the large, suspended room. Three women already loitered in a corner by the windows, engaged in conversation while they sipped at thick green concoctions from clear water bottles. The ethically harvested bamboo floor cost a pretty penny and had delayed the opening of Janna's studio, but she had insisted that they were key to this room in particular. *They are nice.* I particularly admired how darker rectangles, arranged in neat rows, identified where members could place their mats and maintain a safe distance from other patrons.

Click-clack. Janna pressed on a wall panel that turned out to be a well-camouflaged door to a storage room. She grabbed some resistance bands and held them out to me. Each band had *Powerhouse Studio* imprinted on it along with Janna's logo, a woman's silhouette balanced on her posterior with hands and feet extended forming a "V."

"I need one of these by each space for the first two rows," Janna said.

I came to help, but it soon turned out that she didn't need me. The three women who had been conversing also helped, making the setup quick work.

"No rollers today?" one of the women asked.

Janna told her, "No," then introduced me, but their names left my mind as soon as she said them. *Be better.* I scolded myself. The tallest one was named Dana. The other two . . ..

Janna handed me one of the mats she had tucked under her arm. "Normally, I give special attention to new students, but you aren't paying me, are you?"

I shrugged. "Is there a free trial?"

"Get in the back corner, by the window." Janna winked. "Don't cause trouble."

I rolled out my mat and sat down on it. The other women had taken off their shoes, so I did the same, but they weren't sitting. I stood and desperately tried to find a place for my hands as students matriculated into the room. I didn't recognize anyone until Anne walked in, followed by David.

"Yes," I whispered, thankful to have some friends. I knew they took her class, didn't I? I fought back my shame again and tried to focus on how grateful I was that Janna had their support or, even better, they found genuine value in what Janna offered. I sought Janna out within the growing crowd. Surrounded by energetic people, Janna grinned widely, as did everyone else.

"Gideon," David shouted, drawing some brief sharp looks. He lowered his voice, but still spoke a little too loudly for the space. "You're taking the class." He grabbed my arm and gave it a friendly shake. Finally, lowering his voice, David said, "It will be nice not being the only man here."

"Will him being here make you feel more manly?" Anne mocked him from behind.

"No," David said curtly. "It's just nice having a bro around. It's not my fault that most men don't know how hard this stuff is." David leaned in toward me. "Your wife is a beast. She is going to kick our butts today. Every Monday. You'll see."

Great.

David scrunched his brows and worked out a crooked smile like an idea popped into his head. "But you're back now. Maybe she'll stop taking out her frustrations on us."

The voices in the room began to quiet. David and Anne retreated to the front row. Dave wore shorts and a sleeveless shirt which revealed toned arms just large enough to intimidate me. I rubbed one of my biceps. Maybe he had gotten that way from taking Janna's class.

Janna walked us through breathing and focus, then launched into a "standing roll down." I picked up the maneuver after the second time. At least, as far as I could tell. *Not a bad start.*

The workout circuit progressed, some of the moves were more difficult, some of them not, most of the first row utilized their resistance bands on the *easier* workouts. Janna reminded us to breathe and utilize our core throughout. An exercise Janna called "Hundred" particularly burned my abdominals as it literally meant one hundred repetitions. We finished the cycle with a move called a roll-up. Like a lot of the moves, it seemed simple, but doing it properly took effort and concentration, and burned more than just my core.

"Good job, everyone," Janna said in the same quiet tone she had used throughout the sets.

I expected applause, but nobody moved or said anything. Glancing around nervously, I decided to stay put as well. Unfortunately . . . we repeated the entire cycle.

I can't. I labored and slouched like a child during the first repetitions, but then a realization swept over me. *I'm here for a reason. Clear your mind of everything. Surrender to the moment.* I convinced myself that I didn't have a choice. I had to continue. "Easy" did not adequately describe the workout, but it was easier. If I wasn't smiling on the outside, I radiated joy on the inside. My breathing, my muscles, my heartbeat all worked together in unison.

Occasionally, Janna skipped an exercise and walked around the group to help others with their form. Quiet, calm, and supportive, Janna exuded confidence and skill.

When Janna started the third and final cycle, I welcomed the shakiness of my limbs and the acidic pain in my muscles. She still didn't say much to us, but every word of hers refilled my lost energy. I loved every moment of it and breathed deeply when the cycle ended.

Everyone glistened with sweat. Some, like David and me, were drenched. If a word could sum up the mood of the room, I would have picked "grateful." Smiles and soft eyes frequented the faces of everyone near me. I searched for Janna but couldn't find her through the crowd of sweaty people. Earlier, I had said I was proud of my wife, but "proud" didn't adequately describe my feelings about her now.

"Great work today," Janna said. "For those of you staying for the plank challenge, let's get it over with." She groaned.

Plank challenge?

Anne and David stayed along with about half of the class. Most everyone assumed a horizontal position on the floor with their forearms supporting their upper body and toes, shins, or knees supporting the lower half. They extended their bodies flat like a board, like a plank. I hurriedly mimicked David's form on the tips of his toes.

Janna called out thirty seconds and said we were doing one hundred and thirty today. Sweat dripped off my nose, and breathing steadily took effort, but I still had gas in the tank, and amazingly, the activity genuinely helped me to leave my turmoil behind.

No more forgetful Gideon. No more frail, helpless Gideon. No more sad, kidnapping-victim Gideon. Through exercise, I needn't worry about any of those things. Plus, I had become a bigger part in Janna's life. Tomorrow's pain and suffering be damned. A thought entered my head about the *amount* of pain I would likely endure from pushing myself this hard on the first day. The happiness from this first workout surely robbed tomorrow's joy.

The whole of my body seemed on fire as my muscles fatigued. I had to push through, no matter the pain. I couldn't stop. I wouldn't stop. *Don't you dare stop. Stay on your feet soldier.* A sharp crack accompanied a swift strike of a staff across my shoulders. *I won't stop.*

"Gideon," Janna's sweet voice called like a dream, everything I wanted. "Gideon, stop."

"Dude, stop showing off," David said, a hint of laughter in his voice.

Stiffly, I lumbered to my knees and wiped sweat from my eyes. I blinked rapidly at the crowd of onlookers who stood around me. *Twice in one day. Do I like an audience?*

"Were you working out the whole time you were gone?" David joked, receiving a swat from Anne.

"No." I smiled. "I just really needed this."

Janna's wrinkled brow and slight frown couldn't hide her continued concern. She shouldn't have been bothered though, because I spoke the truth. I needed the exercise and I needed her. I chuckled and waved a finger at her. "David was right." I struggled to my feet, with some slight exaggeration. "You kicked our butts today."

Janna squinted, then gave me her beautiful half-smile.

Industry.

"Thanks for letting me drive." I shut my car door and walked quickly around the back of the SUV to open Janna's door for her, but she had already climbed out. "I only got lost that one time, but driving felt normal. Being here should too."

She pushed her door closed and looked up and down my still sweaty exterior. "You insisted on driving and I didn't want to argue. But, now that we're here, I really think you should have gone home and showered first." Janna assessed her own condition, crinkling her nose. Nobody would have guessed she had just exercised. She seemed so well put together that she could represent the clothing designer as a model. "I should have showered, too."

"You look great, but it doesn't matter." I jerked my head toward the main office building of my company's campus. "We won't see anyone. We'll stop at the front desk, then talk to Margie in security, then home."

She frowned slightly and scrutinized me more. "I thought you were more of a plan for the worst kind of guy."

"Not anymore," I said questioningly, then headed for the building, nestled among several others of the sixteen in the two-hundred-acre property belonging to Bright Futures. It didn't *look* right; it didn't *feel* right, like I'd only seen it on a map or in pictures. I squinted and stretched my neck forward in a vain effort to gain clarity. Being at work, possibly around others, should jar some memories, some feelings. *Damn this fog in my brain.*

As we headed for the front entry, we passed the clock tower and the entrance to one of the biking trails provided for the fifteen thousand employees. Had I ever brought Janna and Millie hiking here, or to the lakes or athletic fields? I couldn't ask. I might not like the answer.

At the moment, the campus was deserted, but at full capacity, it dwarfed the nearby town of Ashland, Nebraska and helped to make Nebraska's newest incorporated town, Cascade Valley, the third largest city in the state—a fact we never failed to emphasize when talking to the city council.

Schools, shops, and hotels sprang up around town well before the campus had finished, betting on the promise of jobs and a company with such a *bright future.*

Every building followed the prescribed trend of university campus design with brick exteriors, large, windowed entryways, pristine paths and gardens all shrouded in trees that I would have assumed had been there fifty years, if not that I'd known the company had brought them all in from the surrounding areas.

As Janna and I walked along the brick path leading to the main building, people began pouring out of the woodwork. We were greeted by individuals and groups, most of whom knew my name even though I did not recognize any of them. *Maybe I should have showered.*

We entered the main building and headed for the front desk, a half-circle, wooden behemoth that could have accommodated twenty people. Currently, only one man sat behind the desk. He watched us enter and talked into the microphone of his headset.

The man flipped his microphone up to the side of his head and addressed me. "Gideon Mossert. We were not expecting you."

"I know," I said, placing my hands on the cool surface of the high desk. "We had a break-in back at the house, and I want to speak with Margie about it, if she's available."

"That's horrible." He grimaced. "I'll alert Ms. Kupp."

Kupp? I think that's Margie. I squinted at his badge. *Tanner. Do I know you?*

"You should have called ahead," Janna said, scanning the lobby.

"I realize that now." I shared in her study of the lobby. Only one other person waited, seated in one of a dozen chairs spread about in the expansive entryway. The bulky, probably muscular man stretched the limits of his black suit and held a briefcase upright on his lap. He didn't look my way, so I peered deeper at his familiar face. A deep scar ran across his cheek. How did I know him? Someone famous come to do a commercial, maybe? An actor or boxer, by his build, maybe.

The loud, hurried clacking of heels on tile pulled my attention to the right, where a woman walked toward me from the elevator waiting area. *I know her, too. Is she Margie?*

"Gideon," the woman said. She smiled, tilted her head, then extended a hand toward Janna. "And this is your wife? I am pleased to meet you, Janna."

Janna opened her mouth to speak, but recollection came to me in an instant and I blurted out, "Laura, how are you?" *Laura Sauvy, Vice President of Public Relations, thirty-one, single, takes care of her father since her mother died two years ago. One gray tabby cat. No known hobbies outside of work.* I looked away, cringing. Why did I think that?

"Pleased to meet you, Laura," Janna said congenially. "I apologize for our appearance. Gideon promised we wouldn't run into anyone."

"Well, it is a Monday. I'm surprised to see people working, myself," Laura joked.

Laura hadn't found me here by coincidence. I glanced back at Tanner who watched us from behind the front desk. He had called her. Why? Was there some kind of problem?

Laura pursed her lips and looked down before addressing me. "I had it on my list to call you this afternoon. We want you back, but we didn't expect you so soon. I would have thought you'd want to take more time off before returning to work."

Something was off. My heart quickened along with my breathing. *Don't freak out for a third time today.* I slowed my breathing, *slow and steady* like in Janna's class. The breathing didn't stop me from wagging an angry finger at Tanner, behind the desk, or stop the words from coming out of my mouth. "Did he call you? Did I do something wrong?"

"Gideon," Janna said, reprimanding me under her breath.

"Tanner did call me." Laura licked her lips.

I gave her a double-take, not expecting her to be so forthcoming about it. Why didn't I trust her?

"You're important to the future of our company, Gideon," Laura said. "We wouldn't be where we are without you and I, for one, want to ensure that you come back fully." She lowered her voice. "When you're ready."

"That doesn't sound like your job," I blurted it out before thinking it through.

Janna glared at me.

Stupid. Be better.

"It isn't," Laura spoke calmly. "But, since I was the first person from the company to see you after your release, I'm invested. I care about your well-being."

More likely, she had a list of potential company crazies that she kept an eye on. *Last negative thought. Quit being cynical!* "Thank you, Laura. I'm sorry I'm on edge."

"Quite understandable." Laura clasped her hands in front of her. "What brings the two of you in today?"

I blinked slowly. I'd forgotten. I needed a moment to get the wheels turning in my head again. "Security."

Laura's face slacked.

What? That wasn't enough. I laughed internally at my obtuseness.

"We had a break-in at our house last night," I said.

Laura gasped.

"It's okay. They only took one small thing and ran off." I glanced at Janna, but cheapening her turtle bowl didn't seem to offend her. "I want to talk to Margie and get her advice on upgrading my security at the house."

"And Bright Futures will pay for it." Laura smiled, a little too widely. "Your safety is important. I'll make it Margie's number one priority."

"You don't have to have her do it. I can do it. I just need her advice," I protested.

Janna gently grabbed the front of my arm. "Thank you, Laura. I'd feel better knowing that someone we trust"—she raised her eyebrows at me—"and someone who's an expert in this area helped us out."

"Of course." Laura grinned, placatingly. "Let's go to her—"

"Gideon. Thank God," a voice bellowed through the echoey room.

A tall man, on the thin side, as if I had room to talk, led a group of men and women dressed in suits my way.

Janna half-retreated behind me. "Sorry," I whispered to her. Since I had told her we wouldn't see anyone, obviously we would be seeing everyone.

As the man came closer, I could make out his features. Short, light-brown hair, a well-trimmed beard, high cheekbones and thick, sculpted brows painted him as a handsome man. *James "Jim" Ferret. Thirty-six years old. Married twice. Divorced twice. One child. Loves everything about golf.* I rolled my eyes upward, questioning my brain. *Is this how everyone thinks? Am I a computer now?*

Jim grabbed me around the shoulders and mock hugged me, not quite embracing me, probably aware of the sweat. "You look good." He poked at my stomach. "Lean." Without glancing at Laura, he said her name jovially and received a snarl in reply. His army of suits lost interest quickly after some friendly hellos and drifted to their phones.

Finally, Jim noticed Janna and scooped up her hand, bowing to her and smiling in such an obviously flirty manner that few people could have gotten away with it. He pulled it off. "And you must be the wife." Apparently, he could also get away with condescending behavior.

"Janna," she said in an equally flirty tone.

I raised my brows, glancing between the two of them. *Did this stuff actually work?*

After a moment, Jim abandoned charming my wife and focused back on me. "I am so glad you are here." He jerked a thumb at the young woman next to him. "I was just telling Brit about a phone call I received. Guess who called me, begging." He spread his hands open, framing his face for emphasis. "TerraFission."

My jaw dropped. Usually, the sales team built things up bigger than they were, but this information warranted excitement. TerraFission ran a third of the nuclear reactors in the United States and built their own systems, competing with Bright Futures in the market. Our systems managed most of the rest of the U.S. So, them reaching out to us, presumably for help if Jim sought me out, would be a tremendous win.

"Oh, really?" I leaned toward him.

"Yeah." Almost giddy, Jim bounced on his toes. "I'm—we're going to make so much money on this. They went down for four hours two weeks ago, and it made the news. They said they identified and fixed the problem, but guess what?"

"They didn't fix the problem?" I understood where he was going.

"Right. They are running systems manually and are bleeding money and resources. They have no idea how to fix it, and I hear there's been a secret hearing and a committee assigned. The government is going to start hitting them with fines and possibly intervene directly if an acceptable solution isn't found." Jim licked his lips and raised his hands to frame his thoughts as they came out his mouth unhindered. "They know you by reputation, even before your recent notoriety."

"Notoriety?" Janna protested.

Jim glanced at her but kept going. "Yeah. So, we can basically name our price."

"Pilgrim facility was the only facility that made the news. I assume that's where you want to start." Laura folded her arms.

Jim smirked, his eyes still on me. "Of course."

"That's all the way by Boston." Laura tightened the fold in her arms. "He's not ready for something like that."

Jim quickly turned on Laura. "We can't let this slip away."

I looked away while they argued. *The work is more important than anything. You have to do the work.* "I'll do it."

Protests from Janna and Laura mixed with glee from Jim.

I couldn't meet Janna's eyes. Why did I say that? Laura was right, I needed more time here. *Father to Millie. Husband to Janna.*

"Can you get me remote access?" I asked.

Jim grimaced so vividly that his chin and neck became one. "You know that's a big no-no. That has to be established in person, onsite." He pinched his fingertips together, likely in reference to biometric authentication.

I scratched my head while Jim patiently clasped his hands together.

Janna brushed the small of my back with one hand and whispered my name.

The work is more important. "No" escaped my lips.

"No?" Jim almost shrieked. His face paled.

"No." I shook my head then smiled. "No. I'll do it, but Laura's right I need more time."

"We can't let this sli—"

"You go." I opened my hand toward Jim. "Buy us some time."

His brows furrowed and he shook his head.

"Come on." I smiled. "Give me some more time to recover." I finally met Janna's eyes; they didn't trust me. *Be better.* I turned back to Jim. "Give you some more time to negotiate a better deal. You said they have no idea how to fix it. Think of how much you can take advantage of someone with such an obviously bleeding neck."

A gleam hit Jim's eyes. "Ever think of joining the sales team?" He bit his lip and glanced away. "My knee-jerk reaction was to say 'yes', but I should have asked more questions and pushed for more than just money."

"Give me a month," I said.

Jim nodded while he talked, as if convincing himself. "If I'm going back to the table with them, that shouldn't be a problem. Plus, even a secret, emergency government committee works slowly." He squinted at me. "You sure you can fix it?"

My quick *no* shot his eyebrows up. "But I'll probably just gut most of it and replace it with my stuff." The second part relaxed Jim's face.

"Good, that will likely be faster." Jim looked over his shoulder at Brit who instinctively hid her phone behind her back. "Looks like we've got some work to do, Brit." He turned back to me. "Anything else before I make this happen?"

"One thing. Non-negotiable." I put my arm around Janna and pulled her close to me. "My wife and daughter travel with me."

Together.

New Moon Coffee sure had Janna's devotion. We stopped back there for lunch simply because I had to try their spicy smashed cucumber salad. To the shop's credit, the delicious dish exceeded my expectations.

I swallowed a mouthful and smirked at her. "I guess we didn't need to shower before coming here."

Janna snorted, then covered her mouth. "How could this be worse than your office? I can't believe you did that to me."

"What?"

"I looked awful."

"You have never looked awful in your whole life." I spoke the truth. Janna's worst day rivaled my best. Even when I had been young and dashing, Janna flew high above me, way out of my league.

"We can't go with you." Janna fiddled with her salad, not scooping up anything.

"Then I'm not going."

"Good." She didn't look up.

"But it might work," I said, formulating a plan. *The work is more important than anything. You have to do the work.* "During my . . . absence, you and Millie settled into a routine. It would be good for the three of us to get away together and break that cycle."

"Maybe." She shook her head. "But I have the studio and Millie still has school. She has been spending a lot of time on math. She'd die if it slipped down to a B."

"I've always been good with math. I'll help her study."

Janna looked up, raising an eyebrow. "Really. You always told her it would be better if she figured it out herself."

I chuckled. "I'm not doing anything the way I used to."

A busser picked up a container of dishes in the background, clanking the contents and pulling Janna's attention, but not mine. She caught my adoring eyes, blushed and looked down at her plate again.

"Who are you?" she whispered.

Chuckling again, I shook my head. "I don't know who I am. I just know who I want to be."

"Boston could be fun." Janna looked at me, scrunching her brow. "Anne would take on teaching my classes, but no. You need more time to recover, and you just started exercising. It wouldn't be ideal to take a break so soon. It takes about eight weeks for your brain to form a new habit. Leaving in the middle could break the new pattern."

"I'm sure you can show me some things to do in the hotel room." I smiled. "Plus, Millie and I can do some big city geocaching. She'd love that."

"She would." Janna straightened her posture. "She's dying to go out with you, but I told her not to push you until you regain some strength." She leaned to the side and glanced over me from across the small table. "Turns out, maybe you're okay physically. You'd have to be to survive my class like you did."

Maybe I am fine. No errant thoughts. No strange anxiety. Janna glanced at me meekly, then picked out a small bite of her salad. Such a small action, but it made my breath waver. Everything did. *I love her so much.*

"How long would we be there?" Janna asked.

"One week. Tuesday to Tuesday to be safe." I planned to rip out their controllers and interfaces, replace them with mine, test, slowly move things into production, then pass everything over to a transition team. "Once I overcome any unique sits and prove it's working, we'll do the go live. I can fix the rest of their facilities remotely. Implementation consulting can take on the full makeover without my involvement."

"They're going to let you work remotely?" Janna leaned forward, wide-eyed. "On a nuclear power plant."

"I do it all the time." I grinned. "Even on-site I'm technically remote in the next room. Heck, I'll probably do most of my work from home once Margie upgrades our house. It's very secure, and it's not like I'm just anybody. I have Department of Energy clearance and use my handprint and retinas to gain access."

"It still sounds terrifying. If there's a way in, then can't someone hack them?"

I scrunched my nose and shook my head. "I assure you. Nobody can get in without a hundred people knowing about it. Everything is monitored, traced, tracked, and segregated. I couldn't break anything if I tried, and I have the highest level of remote access."

Janna responded with a single, succinct nod. "So, we'll have a whole week there." She danced in her seat. "Exciting."

"Yeah." The shopkeeper's bell chimed, drawing my attention to the door.

Michael walked in, saw me, turned to leave, turned to stay, then strolled toward the counter like none of it had happened. I lost him when he turned the corner.

Ogon. I shook off the nonsense word.

"—check out how some of the studios over there are run. Maybe get some new ideas." Janna pushed her salad aside, apparently finished with it and kept talking excitedly. "Millie really could use the change of scenery. We haven't done anything since . . . well in a while."

"I think it will be perfect. We'll be together. I can force myself back into things and when I succeed, we can put this whole ordeal behind us."

Janna frowned and pushed my hand away, that I hadn't noticed she'd grabbed. "Is that what this is? Your dumb forced success theory?"

"Dumb?" I winced. "Not completely. Well, if it works then why not?"

"And then what? Will you dive back into your work and abandon us again?" Janna sniffed and turned away. "Maybe for good this time," she muttered.

"No. Never again." I reached for her hand, but she didn't give it to me. "I said I'd work from home. I think the work will help, but nothing is more important than you and Millie."

Her shoulders relaxed. Janna looked deeply into my eyes. "I . . . I believe you. It's just hard with how things were."

"I know." *Husband to Janna. Father to Millie. I'm going to keep on living. I live for them.*

Her half-smile sucked me into a state of bliss. I smiled back and wrapped her hand in both of mine. Nobody on the planet could match me for happiness. My grin widened when she placed her other hand on top of mine. I stared at our embrace.

Nothing could be more important than this . . ..

. . .the work is more important than anything . . ..

. . .you have to do the work . . ..

Focus.

Millie couldn't stop talking all the way home from school about what she wanted to see and do in Boston, mostly searching for caches, but she seemed equally excited to accompany Janna on scouting yoga and Pilates studios. As we pulled into our driveway, three white vans caught our attention, past the now familiar car that belonged to the off-duty policeman we'd hired.

The vehicles had Bright Futures emblazoned on the side and likely belonged to Margie's team of security personnel. We pulled up beside them. Each had its side door opened and bustled with activity from people wearing shirts with the Bright Futures logo on them.

Janna and Millie walked by the people, laughing and focused on their conversation, while I sought out Margie—*Margie Kupp. Single. Fifty-two. Five foot three inches. Dark brown hair with streaks of gray. Never married. Not dating. Loves football, particularly the Huskers and Chiefs—whatever.* I found her leaning against the passenger door of one of the vans, typing aggressively on her phone.

"Margie," I called to her.

She searched the area, settling on me. "Gideon." She grinned. We were friends, if the memories in my head were correct. We shook hands and made it through the awkward and repetitive talk about my weight and my ordeal before she moved onto my security revamp.

"We won't be finished until tomorrow, but it's a major upgrade," Margie said.

"It's fine. I trust you," I said. *I do.*

"I'll tell the boys not to drink your beer," she joked.

"Honestly." I raised my brows. "They can have any beer they find. I've kind of lost a taste for it."

"What's football without beer?" Margie grimaced so deeply that her chin retreated into her neck.

"Football?" I said, questioningly.

Margie slapped my arm and laughed. "You got that right. I'm going to check on these guys." She shot me a glance before leaving. "It's great to see you, Gideon."

Amid the workers, Janna and Millie seemed to radiate with a free and excited attitude while they looked through their clothes to ensure they had everything for the trip. Every exterior door, with a worker attached, had been propped open, letting in a chill breeze, but none of us complained. Just having the workers there made everything seem safer; Janna and Millie expressed similar opinions. If being a bit on the chilly side made us safer, then we paid that price willingly.

Janna and I rummaged through my clothes for the trip together. It started out fun, but quickly became difficult, with only Janna being amused. She had an eye for fashion that eluded me or, as she put it, she had fashion common sense. I learned that I couldn't wear a solid blue tie with a solid blue suit and that I really needed to bring my black shoes if I wanted to bring a black suit, or a gray one. Initially, I assumed simple slacks and a single sports coat would last me all week, but with her help I had six full suits with dress shirts and ties to match, three belts, and three pairs of dress shoes. Oh, and, obviously, the dress socks matched the pants and not the shoes, definitely not the ties. Next, we started into workout attire and leisure wear for evenings and the weekend. I had enough clothes to last a month by the time we finished.

Margie sought me out while I contemplated how much luggage it would take to pack all of these clothes. "Doug has someone who wants to talk to you." She squinted one eye. "I think he's a reporter."

"Who's Doug?" I asked.

"Your off-duty police guy, watching the drive." Margie spread her hands out in front of her, impatiently. "Doug."

I thought his name was Gary.

"Should I talk to a reporter?"

Janna shrugged. "Not if you don't want to. You don't owe anyone anything."

I smiled at Janna. Everything had gone smooth as silk after my earlier panic attacks, considerably lifting my spirits. "Sure, I'll talk to him. What could it hurt?"

Margie handed me off to Doug, who stood next to a man I'd seen at the press conference, the one who asked the questions Laura didn't like. Again, the reporter wore worn, brown pants and a blue, button-up shirt with the sleeves rolled up. It could have been the same clothes he wore over there or he just knew what he liked and hadn't updated his wardrobe in a long time. His salt and pepper hair seemed a bit more kept, like he'd just had a haircut. He wore a small smile and scrutinized me through his thick-lensed glasses.

"I remember you," I said to him.

"Yes. Claude Theuriau with Metropole," he said with his Swiss French accent.

I thanked the security guard and directed Claude to my patio, where we sat in the lounge chairs by the fire pit.

Claude informed me that he was writing a special report on my kidnapping and that he suspected a larger conspiracy at work. *Probably.*

I assured him that everything I had said rang true, which *was* true, even though I had left out details about the torture. The torture didn't matter. I hadn't told my captors anything valuable, and I didn't want the world to know more about my humiliations.

"Can you tell me about the day you were rescued?" Claude asked.

"Not much. I have huge gaps in my memory." I looked him up and down. Maybe he could help me fill in those gaps. "Are you sure I was rescued? I thought I was released."

"Interesting." Claude jotted notes into his notepad. "That you were released was the official statement and still is, that you were released . . .. But, when I broke the story, I was told by an American source that there was a rescue operation that involved a major firefight ending in over twenty insurgents and two American soldiers dead. They found you, the lone living hostage in the center of it. Six days later Izballah claimed credit."

I only remembered one or two kidnappers, and I couldn't picture their faces. My brain hurt from the effort of trying to remember them. And, with the flashes of memory that replayed like old film, a firefight wasn't among the footage. "I'm sorry. There was no firefight."

"Really?" Claude's disappointment hung in the air, but I couldn't help him.

The rest of his inquiries received discouraging responses as well. I answered them in a cloud, searching my memories for details that wouldn't come, even when I knew the answers. After many, many questions with no satisfactory answers, Claude began to repeat some. I winced with each repeat as they reminded me of my capture—questions without torture still triggered the pain.

"Do you remember anything about the captors? An accent or face or clothing?"

"No." I tightly gripped the arm rest of my chair.

"Do you remember any smells or sounds?"

A mildewy, putrid odor assaulted my memory. "No," I said a little louder.

"Everyone tells me I'm wrong, but I know something is here. Are you sure you don't remember being rescued?" Claude adjusted his glasses, studying my face.

I turned away, part of me fearing that he would strike if I told him the wrong answer, any answer. *It's over now. You're safe now.* "I already told you that I don't remember a firefight." My sentence tapered into a growl, but I had no reason to be cross with him. I recovered. "That doesn't mean it didn't happen. My memory is still foggy."

Claude exhaled loudly then shook his head at his notepad. "I'm sorry to make you relive this." He stood and I stood with him. "I'll find my own way out."

"I'm sorry I couldn't be more helpful," I said.

"Oh, one last thing," he said, like an afterthought.

"Were any of your captors Russian or did they deal with anyone from Russia?"

Russian. Sochi. Ogon. "No." My eyes darted away. "Why?"

"Just another thing my source told me, but I guess he was mistaken." Claude headed down the drive, scribbling in his notepad. "Thanks again for your time."

I didn't have answers for much that he threw at me, but he sparked a million more questions in my mind. Laura had squashed his inquiries at the press conference. She knew something but hadn't confided in me. I racked my brain, but the memories didn't come. His Russia question spooked me more than my supposed rescue. What happened to me over there?

Core.

I awoke, but my eyes were already wide open, dry as if they had been open for a while. Janna nuzzled my neck and draped a leg over mine, like she foresaw my departure from the bed. I couldn't leave, or rather I had a reason to linger in bed now.

Had I slept well? I couldn't tell. Darkness still fought the coming dawn, but daylight would soon win out. I slipped my watch on and read the time, seven in the morning, exactly seven. My thoughts scrambled to my last substantial memory, talking to Claude. Had I shut down afterward? If I concentrated, I could almost grasp images of my family, but they stayed in a hazy cloud, out of my reach, and my body seemed to have functioned on autopilot.

After grabbing my wrist and checking the time, Janna moaned. "Ugh. Time to get up." She took a deep breath, then exhaled. "Are you okay? You got quiet after the reporter left."

"I'm okay." I pulled her in tightly. "He just gave me a lot to think about."

"Like what?"

"We didn't talk about it after?" Weird that I had to probe her for information about a possible conversation that I would have been present for.

Janna snorted. "No. You suggested we watch a movie together."

I watched a movie? Never mind. I need to tell Janna everything. "Well . . . Claude, the reporter, thinks there's something bigger going on with my kidnapping and that someone is covering it up."

Sitting up quickly, Janna wrapped her arms around her knees. "Is there something bigger?"

"I don't think so." I huffed. "Well, that's not true, exactly."

Janna groaned, almost a growl. "You have to be honest with me."

"You know I'd been beaten and starved."

She murmured her acknowledgement.

"They also asked about the reactor. I even told Dave and Anne that."

"Some reporter. All he had to do was ask them."

"Right." I laughed, but the thought had merit. "He probably will or has." I rubbed my face. "Janna, I have big gaps in my memory, and I've been . . . ."

"What?"

"I've been spacing off a lot. Tuning out." That statement wasn't completely truthful. So much for telling her everything. What I'd been experiencing went way beyond spacing off.

Janna rested her hand on my chest and turned to me. "I think that's normal with trauma. You'll get better."

"And if I don't?"

"You will."

I couldn't see well in the dark, but I expected a half smile adorned her face.

Her voice cracked. "Or we'll get you the help you need."

I sat up and embraced her for a long time before she pulled away, saying she needed to get ready. Lying back down, I contemplated my day. *Husband to Janna. Father to Millie.* I sprang up from bed and called out to Janna in the bathroom. "Hey, I'm going with you guys today again, right? School and the studio."

"Of course." She stuck her head out of the bathroom door and added, "Unless you're too sore from yesterday."

Surprisingly, as I took inventory of my body, I wasn't sore.

The rest of the morning blissfully ran by. Laughing with Millie at breakfast. Flirting with my wife over coffee. I couldn't have dreamed of a more ideal life. Best of all, I never blacked out once. Every memory in my mind formed fully without the fog. Was I finally on track, taking control of my life, my core?

After Pilates, I held my plank for a respectful amount of time without any weird thoughts attacking my brain. Interacting with Dave and Anne after class went well, even after Dave swore to me, vehemently, that, if asked, he wouldn't tell the reporter anything. Anne, Janna and I shared a laugh at his bravado, but he insisted on his sincerity and loyalty.

I hung out around Janna's studio for a while, admiring her work, but after a surprisingly short amount of time, with so many eyes on me, I had become a distraction, or worse, at odds with the aesthetic Janna had created with the place. I told her that I'd go home, clean up the house and myself, then come grab her to pick up Millie from school. Janna's eyes lit up at the idea, filling in a little more of the emptiness inside, bringing me closer to belonging here. I loved her so much that I had to pinch myself to make sure I hadn't been dreaming.

When I rolled up my driveway to the house, Margie's crew had already resumed their work. With all of their activity, everything seemed uncharacteristically calm and smooth. No shouting, no hurrying, just happy workers going about their business when they weren't greeting or making small talk with me. Margie wasn't there, but a worker said she would stop by when they finished.

I cleaned up from breakfast, got myself washed, and still had plenty of time to investigate what movie I had watched the night before. *The Notebook? What the heck is that?* I read the description. "A romantic drama read from the notebook of an aged man, telling a story to a neighboring nursing home tenant." *Not helpful.*

I tried to watch some sports television, but none of the football highlights or analysis programs held my interest for long. The names of players seemed vaguely familiar; unfortunately, I didn't seem to care about any of them anymore. I remembered Millie had said she'd been reading Tolkien's *Hobbit* and *Lord of the Rings* trilogy, so I spent some time reading *The Hobbit*. I enjoyed the story, quickly turning the pages, but what really excited me was having another topic to talk to Millie about.

Eventually, I became impatient and left for the studio. Listening to the radio in the parking lot mildly troubled me as I couldn't find any songs I recognized. It didn't matter, and it didn't set me off, which only heightened my already great mood. I smiled and left it on an oldies station, letting the simple melodies roll over me. "What a life," I said in excitement. What a life, indeed.

When Janna finally emerged, she greeted me with all smiles. I jumped out of the car and grabbed her bag. She protested, a little, saying she carried it in, she could carry it out. I shrugged it off and stole a quick kiss.

Janna smirked. "What have you done with my husband?"

"Sorry," I said stoically, "you'll just have to get used to the new me."

She laughed and mumbled, "We'll see," still understandably skeptical.

At least I believed I'd given up my old ways. My top priority going forward had to be Janna and Millie.

"What did you have for lunch?" Janna asked.

"Nothing. I forgot." Why hadn't I eaten? My stomach growled with sudden realization, or complaint.

"I didn't eat either. Too busy." Janna hopped in the driver's seat, while I sat in the passenger. "I'll make an early dinner."

"I can make something, or we can order in."

"No." Janna started the car and backed out of the parking spot. "I've been wanting to make jackfruit "chicken wings." I hear they're great, no meat, but taste just like chicken."

"Yum. Amazing." I sounded more sarcastic than I meant.

Taking a moment to glare at me before leaving the parking lot, Janna shook her head. "You make fun, but you'll see."

"I'm going to love them. Millie and I will help."

"Nah. I've never made it before. I'll get frustrated with you guys looking over my shoulder. Just hang out with each other."

"Geocache," I blurted out.

"Yeah." Janna hung on the word. "But nothing too far. I'm hungry and a hungry Janna is a grumpy Janna."

"Another reason to leave the house," I joked.

We shared a laugh at her expense. I had to stop myself from staring at Janna or stupidly smiling or bursting out in tears from the joy in my heart. They needed to know.

"I'm happy," I said.

Janna glanced at me, eyes semi-glazed. "Me too."

When we told Millie about the geocaching, she bounced in her seat and kept leaning forward telling me about everything in the area and showing me on her phone. We settled on a path that started at the end of our driveway, one we'd been to before, although it didn't jog my memory.

Janna let us off at the end of the driveway when we arrived home, leaving us with Millie's water bottle, a pencil, and our phones.

"We could use the app to find the cache, but I know where it is," Millie said.

I followed her lead on the short hike through the woods surrounding our house, toward the cache. Without much prodding, I got Millie to talk about her day at school, her friends, and the book. She even talked about last night's movie with great reverence and, not to mention, speed. Her words came out so fast, holding me in awe. But, most of all, her face shone when she talked. I hung on every word, feeding on her excitement. *I'm home. I'm safe.*

We stopped at the base of a tree with the half-buried cache, a small rectangular blue plastic box that looked a lot like a reusable food storage container. Millie popped it open and searched through the items, a bunch of small tokens and toys. She pulled out a tiny plastic doll that resembled a little girl wearing overalls.

"We put this here on our first trip. Remember?" She held it up to me.

"Sure." I'd remember eventually.

She grabbed a small piece of paper out of the box and handed me the container. Pulling her pencil out, she scribbled on it. "Name and date," she said, more to herself than me. She scanned the paper. "OMG. Tori Herman was here a month ago."

"Do I know her?" I asked.

"No. She's a frenemy. I'm the one who told her about geocaching, and now she acts like she invented it. Is she stalking me?" Millie scowled.

"I'm sure it's nothing," I said, holding the box open for Millie to put the contents back in.

On our way home, the topic of conversation quickly steered away from Tori Herman and back to the things going on in Millie's life. As we passed through Dave and Anne's property, Millie seemed to have run out of things to say, until she stopped walking and looked down at the ground.

"Are you okay?" I asked.

"Yeah." She didn't look up. "Thanks, Dad."

"For what?"

"For hanging out with me on my weird hobby." Millie started to sway, still not looking up. "I'd started to think you didn't like me anymore . . . and then you left . . . .." Her voice broke into a sob.

I grabbed her, holding her tightly. "No. Never, Millie. I love you."

She cried louder and hugged me back.

There didn't seem to be anything to do but tell her everything was fine, that I loved her, and that her hobby wasn't weird; it was cool. Eventually her crying settled down, and she pulled away, laughing.

"What?" I asked.

Millie pointed at my shirt, and I looked down at the wet marks she'd left all over the front of it.

I chuckled, then grabbed her shoulder. "Hey, don't worry about it, and I'm proud of you, and your mother, for how well you've taken care of each other."

Millie nodded, wiping tears onto her sleeve.

"All of that stuff's over now. We're going to be spending a lot more time together."

"Really?" she asked.

"I promise."

She nodded quickly, and we strode back home, hand in hand, like some cheesy movie. Appropriately, I thought of a movie, because it didn't feel real. I hadn't earned it yet. I didn't deserve them. I merely played the part, like an actor in a movie, and my wife and daughter were so desperate for my attention that they ate it up.

I'm better. I'm different. I'll earn this, even if I don't deserve any of it.

We arrived home in time to help Janna put the finishing touches on dinner. I really liked the jackfruit after all and wouldn't shut up about how amazing it was. With every interaction, I slowly grew more comfortable with the love and beauty that Janna and Millie freely gave me.

After dinner, the three of us decided to read, but we did it together, in the same room, often stopping everyone to share a thought or a particularly interesting passage. I didn't make it very far in *The Hobbit*. I couldn't stop thinking about my girls and how much they meant to me. How could I have taken them for granted for so long?

The next few weeks passed in a similar way, spending every possible moment together with no blackouts and no memory lapses. The improved cognizance could have been due to my regular visits with my therapist, Sofia, but even though we talked a lot, I didn't believe we'd accomplished much.

Millie and I must have logged twenty geocaches over the month, and I nearly caught up to her on her reading. I helped Millie with her homework. Janna cut back on her hours at the studio, giving over classes to our eager neighbor, Anne. The life I wanted had arrived, and I didn't want anything to change.

Unfortunately, I had told my company we'd take that stupid trip and fix someone else's mistakes, and Jim had been calling regularly to see if we could leave earlier at TerraFission's behest. I didn't want to do it.

"Let's not go," I blurted out in the middle of a movie we were watching at home, two nights before our trip.

No. The work is more important than anything. You have to do the work

I scrunched my brow and shook my head amongst protests from Millie and Janna. They actually wanted to go? Everything was so great here. My heart beat a little quicker.

"Are you serious, Dad? We've been looking forward to it."

"It's been going so well here." I looked at them pleadingly. "I don't want to mess this up."

Janna rubbed my back and spoke in a soothing tone. "It's okay baby. We're not going to mess anything up."

"Yeah," Millie said a little less soothingly and a lot more bluntly. "It's all great here in Nebraska, but I want to go to Boston."

I grinned at my daughter. *Father to Millie. Husband to Janna.* Of course, she was right, but a quiet voice nagged at me, told me not to go. The quiet voice quickly succumbed to a louder, more insistent voice that wanted me to make the trip. *The work . . . ..* "It's okay. We'll go."

Flight.

"First class." Millie held her hand above her head, and I slapped it, completing the high-five.

"Do you want a drink?" Janna asked from across the aisle, through the line of people still boarding the plane. "I'm going to have a glass of wine."

I held up my water bottle that the flight attendant had given me. "I'm good."

Millie fidgeted and flipped through the in-flight magazine. "I hope they serve dinner." Her excitement bled over to me as I lived vicariously through my twelve-year-old daughter. She tapped the private screen for her seat and flipped through the movie catalog. "They have the new *Star Wars*."

Had I never flown her first class before? *Jamaica three years ago? Colorado five years ago?* Surely Janna and I flew first class on our honeymoon to Hawaii. As nice as first class could be, it paled in comparison to a private jet, but I had put these luxuries behind me. I didn't want them anymore. Had I asked for these seats, or did Jim do this to butter me up? The events of the last two days had compressed themselves together into a single moment, transporting me to this seat. I rubbed my temples. Had the fog returned? Was I blacked out again? It had been so long.

"Hey." Millie tapped my forearm with her phone. "You're going to love the geocache sites I've picked out."

"I bet." I smiled.

She brought up a map on her phone. "This is by the hotel. There're so many caches." She pointed at a spot. "This one's a puzzle box, and if we drive an hour on Sunday, there's an event at Mine Falls Park."

"Let's do it."

Her face lit up, and my eyes welled up with joy. In that moment, Millie's happiness encircled my entire world.

"Gideon?"

A man stopped in the aisle. Pale and thin, thirties or forties, balding, wearing an inexpensive fraying white button up shirt and tan slacks—I could always spot the engineers, but how did he know my name?

The man surmised my inability to recognize him. "Chris. Chris Jones from com sci at M.I.T." He glanced behind him at the impatient stares from people trying to board the plane. "Wait for me after we land. We'll catch up."

"Of course," I said.

He shuffled along with the other passengers.

"Friend from school?" Janna asked.

Chris Jones. Nothing. No data bites. "Maybe." I huffed a laugh and yawned. Flying made me overly tired, something about the cabin pressurization. "Maybe it'll come to me if I take a nap." I leaned back in my seat, and my thoughts drifted back to Claude, for some reason, with all his questions from before. Why was his story so different than the truth, and why had I waited so long to revisit his interview? I tried again to recall the events that surrounded my release or rescue, but only the hotel I stayed in after release formed my first, solid memory. The exercise exhausted my brain, and I succumbed to sleep.

* * *

I'd been to this room a hundred times by now, but it never looked like this. Old, water and blood-stained concrete walls with exposed rebar, a disgustingly soiled and slick floor with a single drain that hadn't worked since before I'd been born, and no light sources save for what a man brought with him all remained the same. I held the lantern above my head. Everything looked identical to before, but foggy and blurry, so not quite the same.

The *same* man, the *only* man who frequented this room coughed underneath his equally blood-stained burlap hood. I looked down my nose at his slumped form, teetering in a wobbly chair. Even if he wasn't bound, this man wouldn't be a threat. He'd been broken.

"I don't know," the man said. "Maybe a computer decades from now could break the encryption, but if the other safeguards are not met, the dataset, uranium, the plutonium are unusable. Satisfying the checks assembles the dataset. There's no other way." He coughed again, this time raspy from the lungs.

Sick. He's going to die soon.

I ripped at his hood. It resisted—dried blood glued it to his face—but I managed to pull it off, revealing the pathetic creature. *Me.*

"You again," he mumbled and slumped even farther down in his chair.

"You again," I said with identical intonation. Panic swept over me. I grabbed at my wrist, ensuring that I held the lantern and wasn't bound to the chair. *Not in the chair.* The lamp flickered, and I staggered, unable to look at myself.

Gideon. Gideon Mossert. "Husband to—"

Chair-bound Gideon continued speaking with me. "—Janna. Father to Millie. I'm going to keep on living. I live for them." I frowned at my broken form. Surely a man could never survive this kind of abuse. But I did. *I'm better now. This is the old Gideon.*

Day in and day out I sat there, a broken shell of a man. That I had returned to this horrid room in a dream didn't ease the shame that the ordeal welled up inside of me.

I dropped to my knees in front of my past self, placing my hands on his lap, his cold lap. "I'm sorry."

"Why?" he asked. A bubble of blood formed in the corner of his mouth.

"You know why," I said. Standing, I ran my hands down the front of the jumpsuit I wore, the clothes of my torturer. Strange that I saw myself as the antagonist in this version of the story. Did I believe everything that happened to me was my fault? Was I the author of all my pain? The face of my true tormentor eluded my memory. I couldn't remember him, or her. The pain remained in my brain but not the architect of my punishment.

I punched the bound version of me in the stomach. The two of us screamed in agony, in unison, identically. "What building do you work in? Which floor?"

"Twenty-nine hundred building, second floor," we both cried out the words.

"What was the last thing you said to your mother?" I slapped the sad version of me across the cheek, feeding on the violence, spitting, and growling as I said the words.

"I don't know. She died years ago. Alone," we said with a hint of defiance in the face of despair. This answer pained me differently as I uncontrollably beat myself up. I couldn't go back and be a better son. *I'll be a better husband, a better father.*

"Tell me the story of when your child came into the world," I screamed an inch away from my face.

The man in the chair mumbled, "Millie," then sobbed. I had to slap him four more times before he recounted the story. Broken Gideon spoke in a monotone as if he were reading a book aloud about his excitement and anxiety, about Janna being induced, about the problems with the breech and umbilical cord, about how he learned to smile from Millie's infectious smile, and about how his daughter cried and cried until he told her everything was okay.

"And?" I asked.

After a pause, the man couldn't help but ruin his beautiful story. We could never see what was important, even when we held it in our arms. "And then . . . I took a work call and went back to the office."

I kicked old Gideon in the chest, knocking the chair backward onto the slimy floor. We deserved it. Straddling him I lost control, punching him in the chest and stomach repeatedly. He spat blood in my face. I laughed and shook him violently. "What's your dream car, Gideon? Who's your celebrity crush?" My maniacal laughter filled the tiny room. I didn't wait for an answer to any of the stupid, meaningless questions that had plagued me every day. Like an animal, I raised both fists above my head and brought them down repeatedly, everywhere I could, until he stopped moving. He deserved it. *I deserve it.*

* * *

A needle jabbed my arm. The room turned bright, too bright to make out anything but the shadow of a man, sitting across a table from me. My body ached, and I wobbled with weakness. I covered my head with my arms and crouched over the table, seeking the comfort of darkness that couldn't exist with this burning light.

"Et'jest. Departure," a man barked out in a familiar baritone. *Russian? No.*

"Voskresheniye. Resurrection."

Stop. "Stop," I muttered.

"Vozrozhdeniye. Revival." The man kept on, ignoring my continued, weak protests. "Zhizn. Living. Bezopasnost'. Safety. Bessmyslennyy. Senseless. Lluchshe. Better. Promyshlennost'. Industry. Vmeste. Together. Fokus. Focus. Jadro. Core. Polet. Fli—"

* * *

I jerked upright in my seat, startling Millie.

"You're okay, Dad. We're starting our descent," she said.

I nodded, then slumped back in my seat. *That was Michael's voice, from the coffee shop.* I rubbed my forehead trying to massage my brain into normal thinking. Had I dreamt at all since I'd been freed? *I don't think so.* Stupid, silly dreams always mixed reality with stray thoughts and whims. Michael and the reporter bringing up Russia, a month ago, must have made some kind of deep impression, invading my subconscious. Russia was a heck of a coincidence, but Michael had said he wasn't from Russia. But he was. From Sochi.

Millie pointed out the small oval window. "Their trees look just like ours."

Following Millie's prompt, I stared listlessly out the window, not appreciating the trees. Of course, the Russian man invaded my dreams. I freaked out in front of him. The torture, though, I tried to not ever think about my torture, but I had no control over dreams. I shivered, and not from the chilly air in the cabin. Something about the nightmare frightened me more than being reminded about my imprisonment. Every time they struck me, every time they starved me, every time they humiliated me, every time they confused me with their questions, one thing rang true– I was a victim.

In my dream, though, I had been both the victim *and* the attacker. Being the assailant didn't sicken me as it should have. Being in control, surrendering to my impulses, and punishing a person I hated didn't bring me joy, but neither did it give me sorrow. Part of me admired the villain in my story, and that was what frightened me the most.

Preparation.

Janna shoved her shoulder bag into my gut. "Here. I'm not carrying everything."

I smiled and looked around my downtown Boston surroundings, then at the pile of bags at the curb. "I'll get the rest." I grabbed another bag and allowed my experiences to catch up. Apparently, I had gone into zombie mode again. The landing, the crowded airport, the tunnel, and our driver, Arnold, not being able to find a good enough spot for the limo came back to me. Arnold helped us unload our bags to the sidewalk, but he really couldn't stay parked here without getting a ticket.

The traffic roared and the constant wind between the tall buildings made me long for my quiet Nebraska town. "It's so noisy."

"Oh, are you awake now? Making small talk?" Janna smiled her adorable half-smile. "You've been a robot for the last hour."

Millie laughed and extended the handle on her roller bag.

"I know," I said.

"You were so rude to your college friend. Millie and I just stared at the floor, hoping it would end."

"Chris?"

"That was it," Millie said excitedly. "We couldn't remember, and you never said it. You barely said anything to him." My daughter frowned. "You can be a dork sometimes."

"I know." I shrugged, then repeated it again more resolutely. "I know."

"He acted like you'd been friends. You're sure you don't remember him?" Janna shook her head. "Or maybe he just exaggerated your relationship because he saw you on the news."

Searching my brain yielded nothing about Chris Jones. "I don't know. Maybe." Why *don't I remember him?* Teachers, adjuncts, other faculty, my transcript, and an ex-girlfriend or two ran through my head like I dug them out of a file cabinet, but no file existed for Chris. What else had I forgotten? The gaps didn't seem to be anything major. Even the details of the ordeal had started to come back. So, I just needed to force my way through this, surrender to my success.

I leaned back, taking in the twenty-five-story hotel. I had stayed in bigger, but this one loomed over the smaller buildings in the seaport district. There had to be over a thousand rooms, all fancy suites for sure, in this modern, newly finished building. Location had been important to me, so Jim picked a hotel close to the harbor, the expo center, downtown, and shopping. When I needed to leave for work, I didn't want Janna and Millie being bored and feeling abandoned.

With some difficulty, I managed to strap two more bags around my shoulders and gripped the two larger roller bags. Millie and Janna only had one small roller to contend with. Before we got to the door, a young woman wearing black shoes and pants, a burgundy hat and matching shirt with too many gold buttons on it, greeted us.

"Welcome to the Ahmny Hotel. I'm Tammy. May I take your luggage?" she asked.

Assessing how I struggled with the bags, how could someone half my frailer-than-normal size manage?

She nodded toward the ground at her feet. "Just leave them here. We'll take care of them."

Janna and Millie retracted the handles on their roller bags. I couldn't shrug under the weight of my bags, but I shrugged on the inside, then dropped them all in a heap next to my family's.

"Thank you." I rummaged in my pocket and handed her a tip, self-conscious about how much. Was it enough? Too much?

Her wide grin told me it was too much. "We'll be right behind you sir."

The lobby of the hotel certainly meant to impress. Gleaming marble floors and pillars gave the area a palace vibe. Men and women wearing suits and such, dressed for important business, sat attentively in the abundant, spacious chairs and mingled on the large rugs that could have been works of art in a museum. Gigantic, old-style paintings depicting notable events of Boston American history, hung throughout, framed in ornate, golden frames meant to look antique. Interestingly enough, the most famous event in my mind, the "Massacre," did not attend the gallery, and the picture of the "Tea Party" showed it as a high class, friendly affair.

No line at the front desk hindered our check-in. Only one person crossed our path on the way, an out of place teenager or very young adult who wore a black sweatshirt, its hood only partially covering his bright red hair. His face bore a frozen smirk identical to Mr. Spencer's from the limo right after my being released from captivity. "Special advisor to the White House" my butt, FBI or CIA, for certain, but not a special advisor. *Can't be him. He had mouse hair.* Would Mr. Spencer now haunt my dreams? *Please, no.*

Tammy and another porter waited for us to finish check-in with all of our luggage on a cart.

"What do you two want to do for dinner?" I asked my girls on the way to the elevator.

"We should probably do some seafood, get some chowder, am I right?" Janna said.

"Well . . .." Millie held up her phone. "There's a French restaurant nearby that looks pricey, but really cool."

What is French food, anyway? *Not french fries. Croissants? Fondue?* Coq au Vin came to mind for some reason, whatever that was.

Hands on hips, Janna tilted her head at Millie. "You're in the mood for French?"

"If you're talking about Benton, it's amazing," Tammy said.

"Yes. Benton." Millie grinned.

"And how do you know about Benton?" Janna interrogated Millie. My wife must have really wanted chowder.

"I looked it up." Millie angled her phone screen toward Janna. "It has good reviews." She lowered her phone and mumbled, "And there's a geocache in the parking lot."

Janna sighed. "You nerds are going to force your hobby on me, aren't you?"

"Two birds with one stone." I held the elevator door open for everyone, waiting to go in last. "But, has anyone ever tried to hit a bird with a rock?"

"Gideon, stop," Janna pleaded.

"I know." Millie chuckled, picking up on my joke. "That makes hitting two birds seem really difficult and killing them near impossible."

The two porters politely laughed along with our banter while Janna covered her face.

"And what's with all the cat skinning?" Millie asked.

"It's an awful thing," I said flatly, quieting everyone in the elevator except for Janna, who groaned. "There's really no sense in it. Killing a cat is bad enough, let alone skinning it. Though, there really does seem like there's only one way to do it."

Again, everyone laughed but Janna.

"Why would you even need more than one way?" Millie asked, raising her voice to be heard over the porters' laughter. "And if you knew another way, why would you go around telling people there's more than one way to do it?"

We arrived on the top floor and exited, all smiles, even Janna. We'd won her over.

The male porter, who hadn't introduced himself, pushed the cart with both hands and turned to Millie, speaking in a low voice,

"Honestly, I want to know who all these monsters are out there beating dead horses."

Millie snorted, then her eyes popped out of her head. She walked stiffly down the hallway, blushing. *So cute.*

I hadn't really looked at him. Dressed identically to Tammy, almost my height, chiseled jaw, and except for the baby-blue eyes, he could have played a younger version of my neighbor David in a movie. *What a handsome young man. Good for him.*

Glancing quickly at him, Millie's lips curved.

Oh no. I strained my neck to get a good look at his nametag. *Ethan. I'll kill him.*

Slowing my pace, I shook my head. *Okay brain. Settle down.*

Ethan looked back at me. Hopefully, I didn't glare at the poor boy. He then regarded my daughter, smiling. My "dad radar" may have been malfunctioning, but it didn't hurt to exercise caution. Still, Millie's height made her seem older. I couldn't embarrass her, but I definitely snarled at him behind his back. *Ethan.*

We arrived at the double-doors to our room. It had its own doorbell. My sales guy, Jim, really wanted this job to go well, didn't he? I opened the door and walked into the entryway, barely getting a glimpse of the room before Millie pushed past me.

"What the heck, Dad?" she asked.

Suddenly, my house back in Nebraska didn't seem extravagant anymore. Floor to ceiling, curved panoramic windows awed me at first with their display of the Boston skyline and part of the bay.

Millie ran into the room, and turned the corner, talking so fast that I couldn't understand her.

Janna eased in next to me and wrapped my arm with hers. "It could use a coat of paint, but it will do."

"Yeah," I gasped.

The first room matched the fashion of the lobby, with marble floors and pillars, but managed to be slightly more intimate with only eight lounge chairs, all facing a low, round table in the center. Beyond that, by the window, a modern, sleek black dining table looked to seat twelve, five on each side, and one at each end.

"There's a screening room," Millie yelled from the right or left. Her echo bounced between the two.

"Would you like us to send up someone to unpack for you?" Tammy asked.

"No." Janna flipped around. "No, thank you."

I handed Tammy another tip and thanked them both, only adding a slightly evil stare for Ethan. They left.

"Well, I guess I know why you travel so much," Janna said.

"We have a hot tub on the balcony." Millie's voice couldn't hold its high pitch for much longer. "I didn't bring a swimsuit."

I shrugged, somewhat guiltily, at Janna. "This isn't normal. Jim thinks if this goes well, then it will land him the biggest sale of his life." I scanned the room. Sure enough, a large gift basket graced the buffet next to the dining table. I jerked my chin in its direction. "See."

"That's nice of him," Janna said, leading me over to it. She grabbed the card. "'Knock 'em dead.' Signed, 'Jimbo.'" She scrunched her nose. "He goes by Jimbo?"

I snickered. "Maybe he's trying it out."

Next to the basket, an ornate crystal bottle, containing a clear liquid also had a card attached. I grabbed the note and read it aloud. "'Neither fluff nor feather.' No signature."

"Is that vodka? It looks expensive," Janna said.

I lifted the bottle up. "Kors Vodka. Yeah."

"I think those go for like ten grand. I saw a thing about it. Maybe it's one of the cheaper ones." Janna removed her phone from her handbag.

The bottle seemed expensive, heavy like real crystal, but the gold inlays could be fake.

Janna gasped. "That is a twenty-thousand-dollar bottle of vodka you are holding." She elbowed me. "Jimbo really wants you to be happy."

"Jimbo would have signed it, taking credit." I licked my lips, suddenly desperate to drink some of the way-too-pricey alcohol. Would I spit it out, like I did my *favorite* beer? I'd never had this brand, but its aroma, like baked bread, washed over me even with the bottle sealed. A sweet, spiciness that many described as bitter, but I found smooth and clean, filled my mouth and ran down my throat, never harsh and never tasting like used dishwater as most popular vodkas did to me. I held up the bottle, squinting at its contents. *The tsar's vodka.* "Da."

"Da," Janna repeated in a poor imitation of Russian. "In Soviet Russia, the vodka drinks you."

Not funny. I shook off the thought and laughed. Janna's joke *was* funny. I sat the bottle down and turned to her. "Let's freshen up and go to dinner."

* * *

I sat my fork down on the white, linen tablecloth. *Dammit.* I squeezed the memories out of my head again. We walked here from the hotel while the sun set. Millie found the geocache and we signed the log. I teased Janna that it would be her first of many. That part didn't seem like zombie behavior, more like another person had taken control of my body.

The aroma from the half-eaten duck on my plate hinted of chestnut and cranberry. It must have been delicious, but sadly, my stomach was already full of it. I cut off a tiny bite. *Mmm. It is delicious.* I raised my cocktail glass to my nose. Empty of liquid, only a large, semi-melted ice cube remained. *Vodka.* The bottle in the room must have put me in the mood.

Janna and Millie talked excitedly, hovering over Millie's cell phone, about Boston Public Garden. Janna glanced at me. "Do you want another drink?"

"No." I said, frowning. I hadn't wanted this one. Janna wasn't to blame, though. I smiled. "So, the park tomorrow?" I exaggerated "park" like a true Bostonian would.

"Yep," Millie said. "There are so many things to see. The weather should be perfect."

"Too bad you can't come with." Janna's eyes rolled away from me.

I agreed. Could TerraFission wait another day? *The work is more important than anything. You have to do the work.* No. TerraFission had suffered too long as it was and had grown impatient. "I'd better go in. Maybe I'll finish early and meet you somewhere."

Millie perked up. "That would be cool. There are caches everywhere in Beantown."

Mental note: Leave early.

I paid the bill. Jim had told me to use my corporate card for everything, so I did, even though it irked me to pay for expensive meals with my family on the company dime. He had assured me that everything I did on this trip fell under the umbrella of "business expenses." But, then again, he wouldn't lose his job over this, would he?

We left Benton and headed for the hotel. Even with streetlights, darkness won out for large stretches of our trip back. Millie and Janna shot furtive glances at every person on foot, so I did my best to keep our pace brisk to assuage their nervousness. Crime could happen to anyone, anywhere, but the statistics warranted caution in larger urban areas more than back home. Even with the booming population of Cascade Valley, the city had yet to experience its first murder. The Castle family had their car stolen out of their garage back home, but that could have been kids messing around.

Cold sweat shot up the back of my neck before I turned, slowly, to look behind us. Two people, one very large, and one slender, dressed completely in black followed us on the sidewalk; I was sure of it. Memories of being taken attacked my brain, but fear didn't consume me. *No.*

Front forward kick to the chest of the smaller. Spin and duck, avoiding the larger one's grip or strikes. Move inside. Kick out the knee. Head butt under chin. Step inside and behind his foot. Push him to the ground. Block for smaller man. Grapple and overpower him. Use his body to stumble the larger opponent. Strike while down. Disable.

I stopped walking. Janna and Millie kept going. I shivered, then huffed a laugh at myself. *Am I crazy? I can't do any of that stuff.* Running to catch up to my family, I asked them to hurry up as I was getting cold. It wasn't a lie. Goosebumps ran up and down my arms and legs.

"It's cold, but not Nebraska cold, Dad," Millie said, using a teasing tone.

I didn't answer. We had to get off the street.

Fortunately, the short trip to the hotel remained incident free. The porters, Tammy and Ethan, approached us as soon as we entered and asked if we needed anything, then moved into small talk about dinner. I couldn't take my eyes off the door.

The two sinister figures entered the lobby, just as menacing, and wearing black overcoats, gloves, and stocking caps. They opened their coats and took off their hats and gloves. The larger one male, the smaller female. My thoughts went to my neighbors, Dave and Anne, but surely they wouldn't be here.

The woman drew my attention and I had gained hers. Long blond hair rolled past her shoulders, red lipstick accentuated her thin lips the same way her dark eyeliner made her eyes seem bigger. Her small frame matched her tiny, triangular face. Nothing about her could be described as beautiful, except that she took my breath away. I had to turn away. I nervously looked at Janna and swallowed hard, my throat suddenly dry.

Tammy reviewed a map with Janna while Millie talked to Ethan. My daughter laughed at everything he said. *Ethan.*

I turned back around to study the menacing couple again. The woman reclined in a chair, near the door, facing away from me. The man sat in a chair opposite her, staring straight at me. His cold, yellowish eyes chilled me, frightened me to the bone. He seemed fat under the coat, but with it open, his overly muscled chest and flat stomach revealed that he could rip me in two if I got in his way. *Best not to look at his girlfriend, then.*

He kept his light brown hair short like a marine's, almost shaved on the sides and barely any on top. A deep scar ran across one of his cheeks . . .. *I know him . . . from the office.*

Without looking back, I reached for Janna, calling her name. "What?" she asked, a little annoyed.

I pointed at the apish man eliciting a frown from him. I didn't care. *Let him be offended. This is weird.* "That guy, Janna."

"Who?"

I wagged my finger at him. "The big one, sitting down. Do you remember him from the office yesterday?"

Janna stepped forward and lowered my hand. "No. He wasn't there." She whispered to me. "Don't point at people like that."

"He was there. Isn't that a weird thing? It can't be coincidence."

Both the man and the woman focused on me, sharing a laugh at my expense.

Turning me around by the shoulders, Janna talked in a low, grumbly voice. "I didn't see them. Let's go up to our room."

Millie and the porters looked on with pitying faces.

I rolled my eyes. *Chalk this up to yet another time I lost my mind.*

Yesterday, that same man held a briefcase and waited in the lobby of the main office. I'd let the argument go, but he was there. *He was there.*

Constance.

Millie picked out a blueberry scone even though I had told her that an American scone would be the driest thing she'd ever eaten. She nibbled away the smallest bite of the pastry, immediately sipped her latte, then smiled at me approvingly. She hated it.

We arrived early at the *Au Bon Café* just off the hotel lobby. Before six in the morning, the place had already filled halfway. I smiled at Janna. She peered at me through half-closed eyes then lifted her black coffee to me, not smiling. Millie had insisted that they send me off to work and get a jump-start on their day. Janna not so much.

"I should be able to leave early today. First days are easy. I'll get set up, learn the lay of the land, and leave." I sipped my Americano.

Janna steadied her gaze on her coffee, not looking up.

Millie sat straighter in her chair, perking up. "Really?"

"Yeah. Why not?" I winked at Millie.

Her wide grin melted my heart. *I live for them.*

I drained the last of my Americano and stood. "I need another one. We lost an hour coming here."

"Tell me about it," Janna grumbled.

"Do you guys want another?" I asked. They didn't.

As I headed for the counter, the same red-headed young adult from the day before crossed in front of me, making it to the counter before me. He wore the same permanent smirk and black sweatshirt as the day before, its hood partially up. He ordered a double espresso.

Uncharacteristically, I tapped him on the arm. "Hey. Do we know each other?"

With a slight turn of his head that revealed only a little of his smirk, he avoided eye contact with me. "No."

Mr. Spencer for sure. But why deny it and disguise yourself with red hair? Or had I been going mad again? Michael from the coffee shop, the people that *followed* us from the night before, not remembering a friend from college, or the details from my rescue . . . I had doubts. *It can't be Mr. Spencer.*

Head down, I tried to piece things together. These memories of mine ran from me when I tried to narrow them down. I couldn't just recollect; I had to concentrate and reiterate the most basic things. College came to mind because of running into Chris Jones on the plane, but where did I go to high school? *Nixa, Missouri.* It read in my mind like a memorized answer, not a feeling or impression.

"May I help you, sir?" the girl behind the counter, Cindy, asked. "Refill on my Americano," I said and paid for it.

I searched for Mr. Spencer or his doppelganger. He sat at a high-top table with his double espresso and studied his phone. Maybe it wasn't him.

Cindy handed me my beverage. I peered at her heart-shaped face and shy eyes to determine if I knew her, real or unreal. I didn't or maybe I did, like Chris from college. Either way, it didn't matter, so I thanked her and returned to my table. Janna's eyes were nearly closed, and Millie had given up her scone for her phone. Millie regarded me with a smile. *She taught me how to smile.* Janna opened her eyes and seemed to startle herself, sending me her beautiful half-smile. *I love you.*

I sat. Being near them filled me with their love.

"My coffee isn't working. I may have to go back to bed," Janna said to Millie.

"We can go back to the room, but I'm not sleeping. I'll plan out our day." Millie tapped on her phone with the geocache application surely open.

"Fair enough," Janna said, then glowered at her coffee.

"I'm going to tell the car service I'm ready." I didn't want to go, but I also didn't want to keep Janna from her sleep or Millie from her planning. "I need to go in but thank you guys for seeing me before work. It means everything to me."

"Aww. We wouldn't miss it Dad," Millie said.

They both stood, exchanged hugs with me, then sat back down as I left. Mille pushed her scone toward Janna and said something to her. Janna shook her head.

I watched Mr. Spencer's look-alike before leaving the cafe, his eyes still locked on his phone, but he did spare a glance at my family. I stopped and pondered. Does he want something from them? *No. Stop being paranoid and stop freaking out.*

I texted the car service that I was ready. They responded immediately, "Five minutes." *Only the best. Jimbo said so.*

A pang of anxiety rolled over me. *What if I fail today?* Had I prepared enough, or, honestly, at all? *I'm fine.* I understood my controllers better than anyone living on the planet. Interfacing them would be a chore, but not outside my skill set, even though I had never seen the systems in place. I'd figure it out, like I always had. I needed this. *Nothing is more important than the work.*

My goals . . . .. What were my goals? Why was I here? Janna's and Millie's happiness mattered to me more than anything, more than my important job, although a piece of me still longed to be productive. I assured myself that completing this project, in this single week, meant that I would have unlimited time to spend with my wife and daughter. I could even quit my job after raking in this financial windfall and pick up a hobby to occupy my time; I could write a book about my ordeal or something, if my memory came back.

I clasped my hands behind my back, under my backpack, and strolled out the front door to await my ride. *A fine goal indeed. Complete this assignment, then turn in my notice, and live happily ever after with my wife and daughter. The perfect plan.* All I had to do was fix TerraFission's flaws, then I could ride off into the sunset. All I had to do was do the work.

The work is important.

Purpose.

I'm typing. My rigid jaw ached. I opened my mouth to stretch the muscles, and the joints popped from the effort. How long had I been typing? I flexed and extended my arms to chase away the stiffness and scanned the sad room. A bulletin board with last year's calendar set to December provided the only decoration in the gray, dusty office space, which had more windows than walls. The desk that I worked at looked rather like a table. Relaxing, I slumped into the wobbly, worn chair that would have been comfy when it had been new, four decades ago. The power plant or TerraFission hadn't gone out of their way to make me comfortable. At least they had let me use my laptop. That seemed extremely important.

Fine. Another autopilot. Zombie mode for the boring parts of work could be advantageous, but did I phase out before I left the hotel? I vigorously rubbed the sides of my head.

I reviewed my code, simple, uninteresting stuff, with a lot of repeated, slightly different subroutines. Whoever designed the control register criteria for physical interfaces must have been crazy, or paranoid. Everything needed different inputs, sometimes flipped bit, sometimes double-bit. What for? The system operated in a closed loop.

A hand reached over my shoulder, pointing at the screen. "You've got a lot of bloated code. What's this part do? It looks like it could be removed, and all still work." His faint accent sounded Spanish, Argentinian, but I didn't have enough to go on to identify the region beyond that.

"Look, man. I've been at it for . . .." I looked at my watch. *Big hand on the three, little hand on the two. No. Six hours.* "Well, for several hours, and I'm close to being able to test. I don't have time to go through all this right now."

"You got it. I'm just happy you're finally here." The hand retreated. It belonged to Almanzo Cordova, Senior Software Engineer and the top on-site expert for Pilgrim Nuclear Power Station, and until a couple of months ago, a big fan of TerraFission's systems. His breath reeked of the same strong coffee that spotted his half-tucked light blue dress shirt. He needed the coffee. The poor guy basically lived at the plant, manually starting and stopping the subroutines that still functioned. "I need to learn. TerraFission only told me the basics."

"Where are they, by the way?" I asked. After I met the TerraFission rep first thing in the morning, she disappeared. *Lucy? Lisa?*

"I think Lori expects you to fail and doesn't want any part of this." Almanzo groaned. "But that is short sighted. If you fail, we all lose our jobs to the windmills."

"Maybe they have a backup plan," I said, still typing.

"I'm too tired to understand why a company would lose millions of dollars, possibly a billion in stock and soft costs, only so they could say that their competition is just as incompetent." He clicked his tongue. "But I don't get paid the big bucks like all of you."

I inhaled deeply. I really didn't need to apologize for making the "big bucks." Glancing over my shoulder at him, I smirked. "All right. I'm going to wrap it up. You can watch, but no questions, please."

Almanzo mock bowed. I didn't think he was being a jerk. I actually liked him.

* * *

With my arms folded I looked through the window of the control room at the test reactor model. I temporarily lost my balance, as I snapped back into existence and gritted my teeth. The lapses of "me" being in control seemed to be getting worse. At least, through concentration, I could replay and verify that I hadn't done anything wrong.

"Rods, pumps, and pins all dancing on your strings like puppets," Almanzo said through the speaker on the wall from inside the staging room. "The new fuel rod housing is a work of genius. Sodium soup is working like a dream."

Jerking my wrist up, I read my watch. *Almost four. I told Millie that I'd leave early.* My phone only had one message from Janna asking when I got off work. They didn't really expect me to leave early. I pressed the speaker call button. "I got to go," I said to Almanzo.

"You are a machine, Gideon." Almanzo's wide grin summoned a smile of my own. "I could call for an outage on reactor two and move some of your control systems and code into production. I'm sure it's safer than what I've been doing."

"No." I didn't mean to yell and wipe Almanzo's grin away. "It's too risky. We'll run these tests for two more days. I'll be back tomorrow."

Almanzo had been right though. My code would work if we moved my controllers over, but it would take hours. I didn't have hours. I stuffed my laptop in my bag and left without saying goodbye.

I removed my phone and texted Janna and Millie. "Leaving work now. Had a great day. How has yours been?"

My car picked me up, and surprisingly, I didn't drift into zombie mode. I exchanged messages with my wife and daughter on the otherwise uneventful, forty-minute drive. They seemed to be in excellent spirits. They wanted to walk with me by the river even though they'd been at it all day. I genuinely couldn't wait to see them and hear about everything in person. Getting back at five-ish didn't necessarily qualify as early, but at least we'd have an hour or so of daylight to play with.

"Can you drop me off at the Esplanade? How much longer?" I asked the driver. The large man didn't introduce himself or talk much.

"Twenty minutes with traffic," he said in a Slavic accent.

Not Russian. Polish. Mazowiecki. Warsaw. Still, I leaned forward and checked his cheek for a scar. Thankfully, he didn't have one, but why would I think the big man with the scar had a Russian accent? I'd never heard him speak, only laugh. *Russia. Always paranoid about Russia.*

I chewed on my lip and stared out the window. The day had been . . . odd, to put it lightly. Almanzo called me a machine and that would explain some things. I'd never coded that quickly before. I raised my hands in front of me and pinched my fingers together. They rubbed and *felt* smooth like skin. *If I'd been replaced by a robot, would I be programmed to think that it feels like skin?* I squeezed harder, making fists, and driving my fingernails into my skin. It hurt. *But, maybe, I'm a really advanced robot. One that gets hungry, and uses the bathroom, and gets excited when his wife grins at him.* I chuckled.

"Joke?" the driver asked.

"Not really." I released my grip. "I'm just stuck in my head. It's been a crazy busy day."

"Too bad. I could use a joke," he said.

"A Polish woman goes to the eye doctor," I blurted out, then face palmed.

He jerked his head to the side. "Go on," he growled.

Why did I do this? Where did the joke even come from? I let the words come out. "They do the eye test. The chart has random letters on it: C Z E N S T A C Z."

I licked my lips. He didn't say anything.

"The doctor asks her if she can read it." My neck froze in place, and I started sweating. The punch line, now that I scrutinized it, was pretty insensitive, even if not as offensive and low effort as most of the jokes that poked fun at his nationality. I'd really painted myself in a corner, though. I cleared my throat. "The woman says, 'Read it? I know him. He's my brother.'"

The vast vacuum of space contained more sound at that moment than the interior of our car.

"You know what?" the man asked.

"I'm sorry," I said, mustering my meekest voice.

"My father's name is Czeslaw, and he would have found that very funny." The man's laugh bellowed, filling the once vacuumous cabin.

I laughed along—respectfully. "I'm . . . .." My name jumbled in my head. It ran from me like some stranger's that I'd just learned and immediately forgotten. *Gidjeon. Gideon.* "I'm Gideon."

"I am Pawel, with a W," Pawel said, letting his laughter taper. "Do you know any other jokes?"

Another *Polish* joke sprang to my mind about going through Polish customs, but he didn't say, "Tell me another Polish joke."

"No," I said, quitting before I offended, if I hadn't already. And what was with all the humor lately? Had I always thought of myself as funny?

"You actually remind me of my father," Pawel said.

"Oh?"

Pawel eyed me in the rearview mirror. "My father had that same distant look in his eyes. He was a soldier, and I think he lived in the past too much. I'm glad you told the joke, Gideon, to keep you in the present. Now, in this moment, is where you can make a difference."

I did think about the past way too much. "Thank you, Pawel."

The rest of the trip, Pawel opened up about his life, growing up in Warsaw, in the neighborhood of Gocławek. He assured me there was no better food in the world, and that, believe it or not, the best pizza in the world existed a block away from where he'd grown up. All the talking about food made my stomach growl. I craved meat dumplings. *Some Pelmeni would be good.*

We entered the Esplanade, and I asked Pawel to pull over and drop me off anywhere. He did and I thanked him. He gave me his card and said he would like to drive me all week, if I could request it. "That would be nice," I said and meant it.

I pulled out my phone and looked at the screen. Nothing new from Janna or Millie had come in, so I started sending them a message. Walking without looking wasn't a great plan. I almost ran into a jogger. The woman's shoes skid on the pavement in front of me. She threw her hands up, huffed, then ran off. Something bounced off my shoes.

Just a mitten, but the woman would likely miss it. I grabbed the mitten and yelled after her. She didn't turn around, likely she had headphones in her ears, so I ran to catch up, even though chasing a woman in the park didn't have the greatest optics.

Right before I caught up to her, she turned on the path past the restrooms . . . and stopped suddenly, almost making me run into her.

I reached with as nonthreatening of a hand that I could conjure, but it still seemed as though I had been about to touch a hot stove. She didn't react.

"Miss. You dropped your glove back there," I yelled in case her music was playing loudly.

A force pushed all the air from my lungs before I pieced together that I'd been grabbed from behind. I struggled to break free and look behind, but I couldn't do either. "Run," I screamed at the woman.

"Easy now. We are friends," a deep voice purred in my ear, a little too familiarly, and, *dammit*, with a Sochi Russian accent. The attacker raised me off my feet. I kicked and fought.

"Help!"

The woman finally turned around; the glint of a small pistol caught my eye. "Quiet, *Gideon*, you'll ruin everything." *Of course, also Sochi.* Long blond hair rolled past her shoulders, red lipstick, dark eyeliner and a tiny, not beautiful, triangular face matched her small frame.

I nodded. The monster behind me loosened his grip and set me back on my feet. *Now is my chance. Grab her wrist, twist it back to the man, who likely has a deep scar on his cheek. If it goes off, great. Pull the gun away and run.*

"Don't make me shoot you *Gideon*." She spat my name and wagged the gun at me, below the waist. "Director Sidorov will be cross if there are delays. Especially when we are so close."

She doesn't want to shoot me. I can work with that. "What do you want, and why have you two been following me?"

"I have all of the answers, *Gideon*."

Why did she gag on my name? People loved my name. She pulled out a needle and the man behind me grabbed me around my neck and covered my mouth with his other hand. I struggled, but he didn't budge. The man had locked around me like steel.

I kicked and flailed at the woman with my free limbs.

"Stop," she said, slicing a dismissive hand in my direction. "You have memory problems, no? You have thoughts that are not your own?"

I slowed my flailing, settling on a single hand, palm out, to harry her.

"This will fix everything that was done to you in the desert."

"What?" I tried to say from behind the man's hand, but only a groan escaped. I relaxed in a sudden slump that required my attacker's support.

Seizing the moment, the woman jabbed me in the neck with the needle while I still considered how terrifying that prospect would be. She sheathed the needle and grinned widely, *not* not beautifully. "See you soon, lover."

My eyes bulged as she ran off, laughter filling the Esplanade. The man discarded me, shoving me to the ground and left, surprisingly silently—or still hovered over me. I dared a quick glance behind, confirming his departure, then stood and wiped leaves and dirt from my pants and shirt.

Calmly, I scanned the terrain for anyone. Maybe they had a sedative in whatever concoction they put in me, because my heart rate remained steady, and I didn't care that I'd been attacked. Definitely, some kind of sedative. With all my anxiety over the past few days, my mind eased. *Lover though. Whatever.*

My phone alerted me. "You here?" Millie sent the message. I responded with my location, and she asked for me to stay put; they knew the spot.

I waited. *What? I've been attacked, jabbed with a needle, and I'm just going to go about my day?*

"Yep," I said.

What about Janna and Millie? Aren't they in danger? The two Russians said they were friends. *Friends don't stalk people and stab them with needles.*

I rubbed my face. *I'm talking to myself like a crazy person.* How had this become the life of a boring engineer from the Midwest? They stabbed a needle . . . in my neck. *Who knows what they put in me? I'm probably dying.*

"I signed seven logs today," Millie yelled.

Peering through my fingers, I watched the two of them walk toward me, almost skipping, and all smiles. I dropped my hands to my side and walked to meet them. Nothing mattered more than them. My two attackers escaped to the back of my mind, filed away with all the other activities that I had drudged through without any awareness. I didn't care that the drugs probably made me not care about any dangers. *What an obtuse thought.*

Janna's forehead creased as I neared. "Are you okay, honey?" She grabbed my arm.

Her warm hand chased away the chill autumn air. The only thing that I wanted at that moment was to remove the worry from her eyes, from her life. My heart beat faster in defiance of whatever drug lurked in my system; my chest seemed to cave in, making breathing difficult around her. I grinned, unrestrictedly, with my whole face.

"I love you," I blurted out, not answering her question. *Okay? I'm way better than okay.*

"I love you too," Janna said, pulling me closer and playfully giggling. Surely, I'd heard her say the words since I'd been back, but I couldn't recall the words ever sounding so sweet. I kissed her.

"Ew, stop," Millie said. She twirled away from us. "Get a room."

"We have a room," Janna said.

"Oh God, no." Millie mock gagged.

Janna and I shared a sinister giggle but stopped the public display of affection.

My incident moments before . . .. *What incident?* As the moments passed, the conflict became more and more distant, intangible.

I tilted my head at Janna. "So, are you a geocacher now? Did you BYOP?"

"It's not that bad." She smiled at Millie, and our daughter mirrored the sentiment. "We had fun. BYOP?"

"Bring your own pencil, Mom," Millie said.

"I understand if it's your thing, though." Janna lowered her chin and looked up at me. "Millie and I have plenty to do together. I don't need to steal your hobbies."

"It's great that you finally joined in." I scooped both of them into a three-way hug. "We can do it together. Stash some caches of our own."

We had only walked for about thirty minutes down the Esplanade before my vision began deteriorating, possibly because of the diminishing light, but definitely the cocktail Sasha and Dmitri administered. Did they put some kind of benzodiazepine in there? They knew I'd been resistant, so a super dose of benzo for me. *Sasha? Dmitri? Benzo?*

I shook my head and grabbed Janna's arm. "Hey, I'm drained all of a sudden. Let's go back to the room, order room service, and watch a movie."

"Yes." Millie made a fist in front of her. "I've been dying to use the screening room."

"Fun," Janna said, with unfortunately a look of concern.
I can fight through whatever this is. For them. I live for them.

Truth.

Yuri scanned the Boston skyline from his bedroom window. He rubbed the spot on his neck where Sasha had jabbed him with that needle in the park earlier that night. The drugs she'd injected had done their work, releasing Yuri's mind from Gideon's grip. Glancing at Gideon's designer watch, fastened loosely around his wrist, he noted the time. *Almost four in the morning. Time to go.*

With an internal sigh, Yuri glanced at Janna. She slept peacefully, oblivious to the stranger, and not her husband Gideon, who had been sleeping next to her this past month. *Everything has proceeded even better than Mikel's designs.* But that's what Mikel Sidorov did. He planned for the worst and hoped for the less worst. This had turned out to be much, much, less worse. *One may even say the best.* Mikel's successes within the United States government had given him the green light for this ambitious program. Doctor Sidorov would have no equal after this. Director Sidorov now, according to Sasha.

Sasha. My love indeed. Yuri laughed quietly at *Gideon's* idiocy. The good doctor's process had even fooled Yuri into believing he was the pathetic failed husband and nuclear software engineer. *Gideon. Gideon.* No wonder Sasha spat out the name. Sasha and Yuri had grown tired of Gideon's boring, uneventful stories that he sobbed out night after night under their torture. The initial feelings of superiority over such a weak man had waned over time, leaving Yuri with only feelings of disgust.

Finding himself staring at Janna, Yuri frowned. *What a waste. I would have never discarded such a woman. Gideon had no self-worth, no sense of purpose. It's a wonder his influence didn't ruin Janna and Millie.* The frown deepened as he left the bedroom.

Men spoke in a room down the hall. Yuri flattened himself against the wall, peering into the hallway leading to the other rooms of their suite. *The television.* Gripping his hands behind his back, Yuri strolled toward the screening room. A peek inside revealed Millie, asleep while a movie played on the oversized television screen, some stupid American science fiction monstrosity about aliens attacking Earth.

The child looked like an angel; a slight smile adorned her blissful face. Yuri gathered Millie up in his arms to take her to bed.

"I'm watching that," Millie mumbled without opening her eyes.

"Plenty of time for that tomorrow, beautiful girl," Yuri whispered.

Gideon's daughter did not protest. Quite the contrary, she nuzzled her nose into Yuri's neck. What an incredible life Gideon must have set aside to pursue work, money, and drink. When Yuri completed his objective, and America was no more, would he be able to start a family and enjoy such a life? He glanced, hesitantly over his shoulder back to Janna's room. *Not with her.* Sasha would never let Janna live if she knew the slightest of what Yuri felt. Sasha never wanted children. *Would Sasha harm Millie?*

Tears welled up in Yuri's eyes as he glanced at Millie on her bed. The girl curled up on her side and wrapped the sheets around her. Yuri tucked the blanket over her as well. *No time for sentiment. Nothing is more important than the mission.* He turned and left the bedroom.

Approaching the screening room, Yuri entered to turn off the television. A woman with light blue skin, standing on the command center of her starship, looked over the earth from space. A strong, imposing, military woman like her should have brought comparisons to Sasha, but only thoughts of Janna came to his mind. A hint of concern, of worry, panged the movie woman's face.

Yuri exhaled slowly and suddenly became uninterested in taking another breath. He couldn't have developed real feelings for Janna or love for Millie. Everything he had done had been fake, a ruse to gain everyone's trust, and obtain unrestricted access to *every* nuclear power plant in America, not to mention Russia's rivals in the rest of the world. These feelings had to have been a byproduct of the process. The doctor would piece these feelings out of him, or possibly eliminate them altogether—if Yuri wished it.

Regardless, it wasn't as if Janna or Millie would even want a life with Yuri, especially if they understood the truth that he was not Gideon Mossert, but just a Russian patriot with a close enough body type to undergo the surgeries and conditioning to become Gideon. At least, Yuri looked close enough to be believable after six months of starvation and torture. The drugs along with the mental conditioning created by Doctor Sidorov had been the latest iteration of many failed attempts by power countries, including America, who had played their games at bringing each other down.

Only, this time it worked. Yuri had gained access to the final twenty-eight power plants in only a few days. Well, it wasn't only Yuri's efforts. Many strings were pulled to cause the failures within TerraFission's systems that brought *Gideon* back to work so quickly.

As Gideon, Yuri had not trusted Laura from public relations, but she may have been the only unwittingly greased wheel in the machine that placed Yuri at the center of this looming powder keg. "Jimbo" had been part of it, no questions asked. The doctor and Yuri had identified key pieces on the chess board of Gideon's life once they extracted a complete profile from Gideon's mind. Many of the pieces, like the TerraFission engineers and a difficult executive at Bright Futures, had already made their sacrifices, sometimes with their lives.

If Laura knew the full extent of what pushing *Gideon* back to work quickly would cause, then she of course would have pulled the plug. *For any matter, too late now.* She played her part just as the doctor predicted and approved Gideon's travel against her better judgment.

Sidorov had many talents and pioneered many fields. With how Yuri had truly believed himself to be Gideon, body and soul, mapping one man's mind and molding it to another's had to be Sidorov's masterpiece, his magnum opus.

Yuri's contributions to the process paled by comparison but did not lack in significance. Prying the actual truth from someone, even with the doctor's magnificent drugs, couldn't be accomplished without Yuri's skills. Possibly Sasha could do it, and a handful of others in Sochi, but Sidorov tended to move too quickly in that one area, without digging past the surface and getting the whole story.

And Yuri had insisted on providing an anchor for his pretender self to grasp onto, a motivator, a purpose that would keep their mind from unraveling. Sidorov's simple ideas of making that anchor patriotism, integrity, or industry wouldn't have worked, in Yuri's opinion. It had to be stronger, a reaching goal or something to feed an insecurity, or both, but nothing effacing that would send them into a hole. The doctor warned against using emotion. He said because of the volatility, but Yuri believed it was because Sidorov only understood anger. The curious, scientific mind of his had relented, and the good doctor vigorously planted the anchor into Yuri's mind, indelible, unremovable, inseparable from Yuri's mind. *I live for them.*

Why had Yuri chosen *love* of all things? *Saying* "I love you" came much easier than *believing* it. Yuri placed his hand on his burning heart. When he suggested the anchor, it seemed a simple one. Gideon had been such a poor steward for his wife and daughter that reconciling that mistake seemed a simple motivator to feed the insecurity and provide a goal to reach. But Gideon no longer lived and somehow a love that never existed as strongly within him blossomed in the heart of his murderer. Not blossomed, burdened. The love burdened Yuri's heart. *I live for them.*

Yuri shook his head at the alien woman on the television screen and turned off the system. *I can't have a life with Gideon's family. It's impossible.* The things Yuri had done for his country would disgust them. The things Yuri had done *to them*, to Gideon, would be unforgivable if they knew. It was bad enough that Yuri knew these things. *Millie cannot know these things. I live for them.*

The thoughts of a life without his wife and daughter froze his lungs and he fought off a sob. *I can't be here anymore.* He hurried out of the room, covering his nose and mouth, forcing the infuriating emotions away. *Focus on the job; the work is most important.* Yuri stumbled, dizzy. *No.* Dropping to a knee, Yuri grabbed his gut. It turned and sloshed. Cold sweat washed over his body. *No. No. No . . ..*

* * *

Rapping on the door, Yuri looked behind him in dismay and grabbed his stomach. *No illness.* He placed a hand on his cheek. *Dry. No sweat.* Sidorov would receive some nasty feedback about his cocktail. Bad enough that the doctor's serum caused illness but lapses in memory simply could not happen, not and maintain mission efficacy.

The door flung open, and Sasha attacked Yuri's face, first barraging his forehead with kisses, then his cheeks and finally, his mouth. She pushed him against the door frame and ran her hands up inside his shirt. *Ah, my true love.* Yuri grabbed Sasha by the waist and lifted her off the ground.

"You did it." Her celebratory smile brightened the rest of her not so beautiful face. "I knew nothing would keep you from me." She laughed and pulled Yuri in for another kiss—and he turned away at the last minute, causing her to kiss his cheek. Sasha slapped Yuri and turned his face back to her.

"What is wrong with you?" she asked.

Yuri's face reddened and his eyes fixed on the floor. "Nothing. Something. The doctor's drugs. I . . .." He glanced at the closing door.

"Let's go see him." She grabbed Yuri's chin and kissed him hard on the mouth. "When a woman kisses you. Kiss her back." Sasha turned and walked deeper into the suite, a suite almost identical to his own. She turned the corner, away from the master bedroom.

Yuri touched his lip. *Blood. Every rose has a thorn, and the Sasha rose wrote that rule.* He followed her down the hall, past the screening room, to a small office or library, a study, which followed the same curved wall design as the rest of the suite. Two floor-to-ceiling, inset bookcases with short, railed ladders held more art than books, although Yuri supposed that could be changed according to a hotel guest's preference.

The desk Doctor Mikel Sidorov sat behind had only a pen, a journal, and a chess board which looked to be in the middle of a game. The doctor gestured to a chair that had been placed on the opposite side of his desk, directly facing him. He tapped his hand on his small journal. "You're thirty minutes late. Sit."

Thirty minutes? Yuri complied and bowed his head. "Nice to see you again, Michael."

"Ah yes. You remember everything from Gideon's existence, then?" Sidorov ran his thumb back and forth on his bottom lip, studying Yuri intently with his unblinking eyes. "I expected that."

Gideon's assessment of his from the New Moon coffee shop couldn't have been farther from the truth. Dressed almost identically, the mistake was understandable, but the brilliant mind of Doctor Sidorov would be wasted as a mere professor.

"I remember everything." *Except the last thirty minutes.* Why did Yuri not share the memory lapse with Mikel immediately? That thirty minutes could undo everything. Still, Yuri held his tongue. "I remember everything from then and before. So, why are we speaking English?"

Mikel's laugh bellowed. "Because my accent gave me away, and I could have endangered the mission. Is it not better?"

"No, it's not," Yuri said, without a hint of his previous Croatian accent.

"Well, then you see that my practice is important work. I made my presence known in Cascade Valley so that I could observe you in the wild, so to speak. You, as Gideon, had a bit of an episode upon hearing my voice. As always, the risk of me being there had been part of my calculations. Necessary to bring you back, eventually."

Yuri nodded and eyed Sasha. "Speaking of endangering the mission, why did Sasha and Dmitri break into Gideon's house?"

Sasha glared at Yuri while Mikel held out a hand to him. "Sasha and Dmitri were there to fix and replace our listening devices." He scrunched his brow with realization and jerked his head to Sasha. "Weren't you?"

"Of course," Sasha curled her nose, leaving out the part about stealing Janna's turtle bowl. *So petty. So jealous.*

It seemed as if Sasha mumbled, "American cow," under her breath, but Yuri wasn't sure.

"So." Yuri touched his fingertips from opposite hands together. "We did it."

"You did it." Mikel huffed out a laugh. "We had six operatives in play before you, and nobody has come close to having your success, let alone move with such speed. And that's not from a lack of effort on our part. But, as my father would say, the first pancake is always a blob. Out of what remains, attacking the electrical grid would reap the most reward, and the waterways project shows promise in spite of the failure of our Pentagon climate expert, another pancake I should say, that has already been . . . disposed of."

Sasha beamed at Yuri. "You succeed where others fail, my love."

Yuri regarded her plainly, then raised his chin to Mikel. "Help me piece some of this together,"

"Do you remember our game?" Mikel gestured to the chessboard. *Chess, Yuri's favorite game. But we didn't play on a board. We played in our heads.* No board existed at the house where they held Gideon, but that didn't stop them from playing chess.

"It's wonderful to see it on a board," Yuri said.

"Yes. The Americans interrupted a marvelous game. Your move."

The doctor had the advantage in the game, but it was far from over in Yuri's mind. Yuri moved his rook from D1 to E1, placing Mikel in a precarious place, deciding between losing his queen or knight at E3 and E4 respectively. Yuri smirked.

"Good move." Mikel rubbed his chin and studied the board as if he hadn't planned for that move, but he surely had planned for it. "But we both still have many paths to victory."

Or maybe Yuri had fallen into a trap. Sidorov's words meant to affect the game as well, hiding a truth on the board. Yuri could distract as well, possibly keeping his advantage in the game, but could also fill some gaps in his memory. "I don't remember a firefight or the rescue."

"You wouldn't." Mikel moved his knight from E4 to F2. "Check."

Check? Yuri studied the board intently. *He's stalling the inevitable.*

"Our sources failed to warn us that the Americans had found the Izballah stronghold we held Gideon in. You were nearly ready, but not fully. I wanted us all to leave and start over, but you talked me into activating you and leaving you to be found by them. That process, as you know, affects short term memory."

"So, there was a firefight?" Yuri moved his king from H1 to G1, out of check.

"Yes. Izballah did their best to help our escape, but they were no match for the Americans. We had only used them to move freely in the area, not for their protection. If not for Sasha, I would have been captured."

"I should have killed more of them." Sasha rolled a fist in front of her. "But the Director made us run away." She smiled at Yuri.

"Why would the Americans cover that up, then?"

"Not every Izballah soldier died. One of them talked, saying the only useful thing that any of them knew." Mikel moved his knight from E2 to H3. "Check."

"Russia," Yuri said.

"Yes. Yes. I planned for that, though," Mikel said. "The Americans didn't want the world to know what they themselves know which we obviously know, so they said you were released so that nobody would question anyone of the military." He gestured toward me. "Bright Futures and the other companies involved were only too happy to not be associated with an international conspiracy."

Yuri backed his king away from G1 to H1, out of check. *How am I now running? I'd won this game.*

"And, although they were very useful, Izballah will never be heard from again." Mikel looked away from the board, giving Yuri the feeling this game was already over. "What do you feel is the next step with your work?" Mikel asked.

"The beauty of it is that I do not need full implementation of my programs in order to execute the attack," Yuri said.

"Yes. Yes. We designed this strategy together, Yuri." Mikel moved his queen from E3 to G1, next to Yuri's king. "Check."

Frowning, Yuri straightened his posture and peered closer at the board. *His queen is protected by the knight at H3, but it's the queen. I can take it with my rook at E1. Sure, he can take my rook with the knight, but . . . he's made a mistake . . . he doesn't make mistakes.*

Mikel gestured to Yuri. "But please say the plan aloud and articulate any obstacles or changes you've had to make along the way."

"Almanzo trusts me and the system. He criticized some coding bloat, but he's too tired to make a formal protest or review."

"We do not want him looking too closely at that, but the routines themselves will not reveal ill intent," Mikel said.

"He won't look at it. I had to hold him back on the rest of it. Almanzo wanted to go live with the initial control systems yesterday. I told him to wait, that we needed more testing." Yuri scratched his head. *I'm doing it. I'm taking the queen.* Yuri grinned widely and moved his rook from E1 to G1, taking Mikel's queen.

"And why did you tell him to wait, my love?" Sasha asked. "We could be finished here."

"I . . .." Yuri rubbed his temples and opened his mouth, but the words wouldn't come out. He beat a fist on the desk near the board, rattling some of the pieces. "Gideon. He wanted to be with his family."

"Not unexpected." Mikel produced a large white pill from his jacket pocket, placed it on the desk and pushed it toward Yuri. "Take this now and take one every morning until the pills are gone." The doctor set a pillbox next to the pill.

"But I'm back. I'm me." Yuri stared at the enormous pill. *I can't swallow that.*

"You are still you, and not you." Mikel moved his knight from H3 to F2. "Checkmate. Your best game yet, *Yuri.*"

Yuri groaned. *Checkmate? Impossible, but just like Sidorov to sacrifice his most powerful piece and still win the game.* The thought made the prospect of swallowing Mikel's pill even more daunting. *Is he sacrificing me?* Mikel wouldn't hesitate to throw his children to the wolves.

"The injection Sasha gave you will wear off in time. Plus, there is more to do to repair your mind than mere chemicals." Mikel tilted his head at Sasha, prompting her to leave the room. "Tell me more of your plan."

"Like I said, Almanzo wants to move quickly." Yuri squinted at the chessboard. *How did Sidorov manage to manipulate me? I'd won.* "Today, I expect to link my controllers through their interface engine to gauge how we'll perform using real time feedback."

"Today?" Mikel laughed. "I thought this would take them months. Sasha was right to think that we could have been done yesterday."

All I would have had to do was blow off Janna and Millie. The delay was worth it to see them one last time.

Sasha returned with a glass of water and set it by the pill. "Take your pill."

Like a child, Yuri jerked his head down at the pill, scooped it up, then nearly gagged on the oversized capsule. Picking up the glass and filling his mouth with the cool liquid, Yuri retched when it unexpectedly burned like kerosene. He spat out the liquid along with the pill, onto the floor.

"Vodka?" Yuri's throat seemed to smolder; he expected smoke to roll out as he croaked the words. "It's five in the morning."

Sasha squatted and picked up his pill, holding it between her finger and thumb. She raised her brows to Yuri. "That never bothered you before, lover."

True. I'm back. I am Yuri. I believe in this plan.

Yuri snatched the pill and attempted the maneuver again, this time without coughing. He then stared, resolutely at Mikel. "It's not unrealistic to expect it to happen today. On the surface, there's no danger in touching their interface engine, and your pressure on TerraFission has everyone desperate for resolution." Yuri reviewed his programs in his head. *The interface engine is vulnerable to attack. I'll control the engine and gain access to their closed system, inject my system loop that looks like bloated code, drop the rest of my code, and initiate the chain reactions.*

"Then it is inevitable, like this chess game. Checkmate," Mikel said.

"A hundred nuclear bombs going off on American soil and all looking like an accident. They'll never recover." Sasha could not hide her excitement.

"No. Not bomb." Mikel sliced a hand in front of him, his face reddened, and his accent came back in full force. "My superiors say bomb all the time. They do not listen. This is worse than bomb. The damage will be a thousand times worse than Chernobyl. Beyond INES seven. The operators at the plants will not even know what is happening until they drop dead. No alarms. No warning. Only death. And Yuri will expose more rods than normal at the sites using his cages. We can only estimate the impact we will have, for not until it is done will we fathom the true damage. The people, the resources, the economy, and the government will all be in shambles. We will win the war without firing a shot and without invading this failed state, not that we'd want to come here after this week."

The only problem is that Janna and Millie live in this failed state. I grimaced at their plight.

"What is it, my love?" Sasha asked. "Will Gideon miss making pancakes for his family?"

Why must she taunt me so?

"The pill will help with that, Yuri. And so will Dmitri," Mikel said.

Sasha snickered at some unsaid joke. *About the pancakes? Dmitri?*

"What can Dmitri help with?" Yuri asked.

Glancing at his watch, Mikel sighed. "I did so like speaking with Janna and Millie, but alas Dmitri must already be finished with his dark work."

"We couldn't have them running around, talking about you," Sasha smirked. "Unless you want another new face. I hear it gets harder to keep you looking human after too many changes."

"What did you do, Sasha?" *No. She couldn't have.* Yuri's stomach boiled and his body shook.

"It was my order, Yuri," Mikel said, without emotion. "They were no longer necessary and only posed problems. Dmitri is professional, not animal. I'm sure he made it quick and painless."

Janna, dead. And . . . Millie . . ..

* * *

"No!" I leaped from my chair so fast that I sent it flying back across the room. Sasha grabbed my shoulder. I grabbed her thumb and wrenched it back. She squealed in pain then bared her teeth. *Sasha bares her teeth before striking.* I brushed away her strike at my neck and applied more pressure, twisting her thumb. I wanted to . . . I needed to hurt her.

"Release her, Yuri."

Yuri? I snarled at Mikel. *I could kill them both, but it wouldn't bring Janna and Millie back. I can still stop his plan, though.*

Sasha moaned in agony.

"Yuri. Remember." Mikel pleaded. "You had to believe you loved them, but you don't."

"Don't tell me how to feel, how to thi—"

* * *

Yuri stared down in confusion at Sasha, who screamed obscenities and cried in pain. Suddenly aware of the source of her pain, Yuri released his grip on her thumb. "I'm sorry, Sasha."

She looked away, groaning and rubbing her shoulder.

"All is well, Yuri. This is expected," Mikel said.

"Expected," Sasha growled. "I'll kill him." She sprang up and, in her fury, threw a sloppy punch at Yuri's face. He easily dodged it. *Sasha still shows teeth before striking. Come on, love, you're better than that.* Yuri tackled Sasha and held her in a bear hug, mostly avoiding her repeated bites and kicks.

"I won't have this, Sasha," Mikel yelled. "You know why this happened. I explained all of this to you."

"Nobody can explain all of this." Her knee finally found a home between Yuri's legs.

He crumpled to the ground, holding himself and wheezing in agony.

"Nobody could explain how it would make me feel." Sasha's voice cracked, then turned to a hiss. "Watching him with her."

"Feelings are irrelevant, Sasha. If I tell him to, Dmitri will protect the mission from you as well."

Sasha's eyes bulged, then she folded her arms and turned away.

Yuri stumbled back to his feet. "I don't even know what happened. Christ, Sasha."

Mikel held a hand to the upside-down chair on the other side of the room and said, "Sit."

The chair had a cracked leg, but Yuri made it work. He sat and faced Mikel while Sasha pouted in the corner, faking a browse of the bookshelf.

"Place your hands on the desk, palm down," Mikel said.

Yuri brushed away a couple of pawns from the desk and complied. *What happened?* Mikel placed his hands on top of Yuri's.

"Departure. Et'jest," Mikel said in unison with Yuri.

"Resurrection. Voskresheniye. Revival. Vozrozhdeniye. Living. Zhizn. Safety. Bezopasnost'. Senseless. Bessmyslennyy. Better. Lluchshe. Industry. Promyshlennost'. Together. Vmeste. Focus. Fokus. Core. Jadro. Flight. Polet. Preparation. Podgotovka. Purpose. Tsel. Truth. Pravda. Conviction. Uezhdeniye."

Yuri stood and left the room without another word, but two names echoed in his head. *Janna. Millie.*

Conviction.

Yuri sent several text messages to Jana and Millie on the way to Pilgrim Station, but they did not respond. *They can't be dead. They didn't matter, though, did they? I can't be okay with killing millions and then get hung up on two people.*

A ghostly image of Janna's half smile appeared in Yuri's head. *I'll miss seeing that.* Millie's infectious laugh haunted him as well; the sensation forced a sniffle.

"No jokes, today?" Pawel asked.

How about this one? If I live for them, then why am I alive?

"None today, Pawel. Unless you have one." Yuri rolled his eyes and faced the window.

"What do you call someone who speaks two languages?" Pawel asked.

Ahh . . . the American joke. "Bilingual?"

"Yes." Pawel had already started snickering. "What do you call someone who speaks three languages?"

"Trilingual."

"And what do you call someone who only speaks one language?" Pawel delivered this line flatly, keeping his composure.

"I don't know," Yuri said.

"American." Pawel bounced in his seat with laughter and Yuri forced a laugh along with him. The car jerked as Pawel's control suffered.

Yuri agreed with the sentiment. The American he pretended to be only spoke *American,* as Gideon had put it when they met in the hotel bar so many months ago.

A text message from an unknown number came through on Yuri's phone, "42." *Odd.* An alert for two voicemails also caught his eye.

Pawel picked up his conversation about his motherland. He didn't require much from Yuri in that regard; only the occasional, "Oh really," and, "Sounds amazing," sufficed to keep him going.

"Where are they?" Sasha texted.

"Who?" Yuri texted back.

"Don't play stupid," came the reply.

Sasha is being a real pain in my ass. After recruiting me and talking me into volunteering, I'd think she'd cut me some slack. All this pain of hers was her own doing. Yuri didn't respond to her message.

He sighed at the long message that followed. What had Sasha in such a mood? He considered leaving it for later but gave in and read it.

"I know you did something even if Mikel believes you didn't. He gave me some nonsense theory about WOMEN KNOWING when something is wrong, and that's why they left, and that he had planned for this, but I'm a woman and I KNOW you told them something."

Janna and Millie left? They're alive? Don't react to Sasha. Be grateful they're not dead. I can live again.

"I didn't do anything, Sasha." *Did I do something in that missing half hour?* "Dmitri will find them." *Dmitri will find them, and that's unfortunate. What can I do to stop him?*

"Do you need help finding them?" Yuri texted Dmitri. Another message came from the same unknown number, "21." Dmitri didn't reply.

"I'll find them," Sasha messaged.

Yuri typed, "Let Dmitri," but erased it. Sasha's jealousy and bloodlust wouldn't bode well for Janna and Millie if she found them. Sasha's violent tendencies and lack of a conscience used to excite Yuri. It had always been them against the world, and they enjoyed watching the world burn together. It wasn't love though, was it? *Something else.*

Janna, by contrast, would help someone a hundred different ways and never think of harming them, but Yuri figured that if something threatened Millie's safety, then Janna wouldn't hesitate to take any action necessary to protect her. Pilates made Janna strong mentally and physically, and the results left her more than capable. Still, Janna would be nowhere near Sasha's level.

The training that Yuri and Sasha had endured with the others in Sochi went far beyond what Janna had subjected herself to. In Sochi, in addition to intense physical training and mental hardening, Yuri and Sasha faced torture, starvation, and fatigue—worse than Gideon's final days—in order to be prepared for and survive extreme conditions. Still, if it came down to a fist fight, even with all of Sasha's combat skills and natural talent, Yuri could not predict who the winner would be, not when Janna had a mother's protective instinct going. The image of a mother bear protecting her cub came to mind. Is that what made Sasha so insecure?

Nothing is more important than the work. I live for them.

The thoughts, the voices, in Yuri's head guided his focus, but contrasted with one another. Was one voice Sidorov's and the other Yuri's? He gripped his phone tightly, torn between being compelled to complete the mission and a desire to save his family. *No. Gideon's family.*

Yuri's breathing shallowed and his heart sank. He covered his chest. *I can't let them die, even if it means saving everyone.* Yuri laughed at the audacity of such a thought.

"Another joke?" Pawel asked.

"Not really, no." Yuri put his headphones in his ears. "I need to make a call."

For most of the rest of the trip, Yuri alternated between calling Janna and Milli and checking the last known positions of their phones with no success. He then called the hotel and asked for the porter, Ethan. If anyone knew where his daughter—Gideon's daughter—had been, it would be Ethan, but he said he hadn't seen the girls this morning. Had they left through a back way, or was Sasha tormenting Yuri, making him believe they were alive when Dmitri had already killed them?

Frustrated, Yuri played his voicemails. The first, from Laura in Human Resources, went on way too long about how he was feeling and that he needed to work at his own pace. She bounced back and forth between the two topics before the system cut her off. Her guilt at sending Gideon back to work so quickly must have been gnawing at her.

The second voicemail, from the reporter, Claude, almost made Yuri laugh, if not for the fear that Pawel would ask to be let in on the joke. Claude had come into some urgent information from an FBI informant that confirmed the reporter's suspicions. *Gideon* needed to contact him immediately, for his life depended on it. *Oh Claude, so close.* But maybe Claude could help Janna and Millie. Or this FBI agent could take Yuri into custody. *Mr. Spencer?* How could Yuri use Claude without handing them all over to Dmitri? *Or Sasha.*

Sasha had a cruel streak, one that Yuri used to identify with. Directing their angst at others had given him pleasure before, but being on the receiving end of her cruelty, especially this mental anguish, pushed Yuri away from Sasha. Was this simply the final straw breaking the donkey's back? *No.* Sasha and he had fought all the time, but they never argued. The two of them had been of one mind. *If Sasha has hurt Janna or Millie . . . ..* Yuri squeezed his phone until the screen began to crack. *Sasha.*

Wiping his face with his hands, Yuri rubbed his eyes. *It doesn't matter. Stop thinking about them. Finish the mission.* "No," Yuri said.

"No?" Pawel questioned. The car slowed in front of the power plant. "Do you not want me to stop?"

"Please pull up to the front. I'm just talking to myself."

Pawel eyeballed Yuri in the mirror but complied and wished him a good day.

As Yuri walked to the front door, he checked the last recorded positions of Millie's and Janna's phones. *Still at the hotel over an hour ago.* He shook his damaged phone in frustration and growled.

"Are you okay?" Almanzo asked.

"Yes." Yuri jerked his head up from his phone and smirked at Almanzo.

"Good. I came out to catch you before going in." Almanzo fidgeted.

"Is there a problem?"

"No. Well, yes." Almanzo darted a glance over his shoulder. "The suits from TerraFission are all here today. I think you've embarrassed them by fixing it so quickly, and they want to grill you before letting you work again." He shrugged. "It's not like they have a choice. You being here, that is."

It's easy to fix an issue when I have a team of programmers in Sochi that provided me with every answer before I even saw the problems. It also didn't hurt that they created said problems through other operatives in the first place. If my biometrics weren't needed to access remotely, then they'd likely be able to finish without me.

Almanzo led Yuri to the third-floor conference room without any additional information besides logistical. Almanzo held the door to the room open. "I'm on your side, but I probably won't say much in here. Good luck."

Upon entering the conference room, Yuri scrunched his nose, not even trying to hide his condescension. *What a bunch of idiots. How could they not see through this facade?* Four obvious engineers, with their business casual attire, hovered over two laptops and several piles of printed papers scattered across the large conference table. Three men and four women in immaculate dark suits hovered over a buffet table on the far wall where they drank coffee or tea and spoke in low voices. Lori, from the day before, wasn't with them. Their bodies collectively jerked toward Yuri as he entered.

A woman approached him, hand outstretched for a handshake. "Gideon Mossert. It is a pleasure to meet you."

"Likewise." Yuri shook her hand. "And you are?"

"Oh my God, I'm sorry." She blushed. "It's early still, isn't it? My name is Marie, TerraFission's Vice President of Technology." Marie proceeded to point and introduce everyone in the room. Yuri did not bother to listen, instead he moved to the table, setting his phone and backpack on top of it.

"Let's get to it. I have a lot of work to do," Yuri said. He tilted his head. *Back on track. Don't think about Janna and Millie.* He closed his eyes. *Great. Now that's all I'm thinking about.*

Marie called on another woman, Chelsea, and asked her to explain their concerns.

Chelsea fumbled with the remote for the large display over the buffet table, then had equal trouble bringing her laptop screen up on the group screen. Once Chelsea awkwardly covered her education and background, she painfully explained what she had been tasked with—finding problems with Yuri's coding.

Yuri looked at his watch and sighed. Chelsea had already wasted fifteen minutes, fifteen minutes away from his objective, fifteen more minutes of Janna and Millie in peril. *I can do both. I can complete the mission and get them to safety.* Yuri rolled his neck around.

"What, you don't think peer review is important?" Chelsea asked, suddenly finding her confidence.

"We have peer review. Our group in Bangalore has over twenty full-time coders with peer review being their only function." Mostly true, this code had been reviewed in Sochi, the only lie in his sentence.

Another number popped up on Yuri's phone, "199." *Who's sending me numbers?*

Chelsea kept on her assault without really saying anything concrete. Everything she had been suggesting wouldn't have made any difference, and she'd already lost the attention of the suits in the room. It was as if Chelsea needed to show that she understood the code and would have done things better.

"Does it matter?" Yuri interrupted.

"What?" Chelsea asked.

"Does anything you are saying matter?"

Chelsea's face paled, then reddened as she puffed up her chest and launched a barrage of protests. Her heated words finally awakened some of the suits who joined in equally admonishingly. Eventually they stopped their questions and statements and looked to Yuri to explain himself.

"Look." Yuri threw his backpack over his shoulder and picked up his phone. "You've all been at this for weeks, and I understand the frustration, but your problems weren't just software related. Your controllers have serious limitations. I'm sorry that my success irked you, but there are more important things to address than this." He stared at Chelsea's raised chin. "Will my code work?"

"We need more testing before we can make that determination," Chelsea said, like a true engineer.

Yuri scanned the suits until he found Marie. "And how much money are you losing every day you delay? Surely someone's going to take the blame here."

Marie sneered at Yuri, briefly, then turned to Chelsea. "Will it work?"

Chelsea's lips twisted into a pained grimace, but she relented and nodded.

"Almanzo?" Marie asked.

"I think it's brilliant. It will work," Almonzo said excitedly.

"Then I think we should proceed," Marie said.

Triumphant, Yuri headed for the door.

"What about the subroutine at line seven-hundred and twenty?" a man's voice asked from the table.

My bloated code. Harmless, until activated. Stopping, Yuri looked over his shoulder and answered. "It's only there in case we need to replace a controller. I can send controllers and interfaces here, in a loop, and replace a device without taking a downtime." *Sure. Why not?*

"No, that can't be" the man said, and typed furiously on his keyboard.

Yuri continued walking, turning forward. On his way out, the engineers' excited chatter confirmed that what Yuri had said was indeed correct.

It's better to be lucky than good. Even though ghosts did exist within the machine, luck never really played a part so well when it came to coding. Honestly, the loop existed, but lay vulnerable to attachment from other code, Yuri's code. Sneaky. Had Yuri actually become as talented a coder as Gideon? The programming languages and scripts played back in Yuri's head. Every line made sense and rang with purpose. Was it like Gideon had said, when they met as friends, that anyone could do what Gideon did, but they just lacked his passion? Or did motivation trump passion, as in Yuri's case?

Someone grabbed Yuri's arm from behind. Yuri moved to disable his assailant but pulled short after seeing Almonzo.

"You really put them in their place," Almonzo said.

"Did I?" Yuri scowled. "I didn't mean to. I just want us to get up and running."

"So, you're ready to go into production?" Almonzo smiled. "Will I finally get to bed at a decent time?"

"I'm sorry, Almonzo." Gideon placed a comforting hand on Almonzo's shoulder. "We are not ready for production. It works here, but I need more data."

"More data? We've thrown five years of alerts, metrics, and baking schedules into your system. It handled it all." Almonzo folded his arms, likely disappointed at being so close, but not close enough to finish. "What more do you want?"

"You know every facility is different." Yuri waited for the expected curt nod from Almonzo before continuing. "I need access to the other facilities. I want to pull their live interface data into this system, to test the expected variances."

"I've seen their flows. There's not much variance." Almonzo frowned.

"But there is a difference." Yuri raised a finger. "People rely on us for power. Plus, we have congress breathing down our necks. Let's be thorough."

Unfolding his arms, Almonzo tilted his head. "Fine. But promise me we'll be done today and move forward into production, at least at my facility, by tomorrow."

Yuri rubbed his chin in mock thought. *So easy, I could do it with my left hand.* "Sure, Almonzo. As long as we don't encounter any problems."

"Of course." Almonzo covered his heart with his hands. "But my health can't take it if we have problems."

The number "71" flashed across Yuri's phone screen from the same caller as the other numbers. Yuri tapped the number and hovered over the "block source" button, but he froze in place. *This is Janna or Millie sending me a message.* Yuri strode toward the front door, but Alonzo quickly accosted him.

"Hey, the control room is this way." Almonzo's grip tightened on Yuri's forearm. "You *just* promised we'd do this today. Shouldn't we get started?"

Yuri nodded and spun around. He walked alongside Almonzo to the control center, deep in thought about what he could do to save his Janna and Millie. *Why are they sending me numbers?*

As if on cue, "4" popped across his screen from the same unknown number.

"Who is this?" Yuri texted the number. "408," replied back. *Maybe it is just random.*

When they arrived at the control center, all eyes landed on Yuri, unlike the anonymity he enjoyed the day before. He must have made an impression on them. What could he say? *I've impressed everyone I've met all the way back to the Kremlin.*

Almonzo updated Yuri on the successful test iterations that had run all night. His labored voice went on and on about how he agreed that they should proceed with caution, even amid the perfect results. The thick sarcasm wasn't lost on Yuri, and had not everything that he had done been sinister in nature, he might have conceded and moved forward at a faster pace, making Almonzo's life easier.

"Let's get the other interfaces going," Yuri said, holding back the urge to add, ". . . and maybe move some of this into production." Yuri liked Almonzo, but he would be dead by tomorrow. His gut wrenched so strongly at the thought of this man dying that he couldn't bear adding to it by getting to know the other people in the control room, and risk liking them as well.

Maybe. Maybe Director Sidorov would call the whole thing off. Maybe Yuri wasn't as talented at programming as he thought. Maybe the Sochi group that came up with the code structure and reviewed everything he had done weren't as good as everyone thought they were. *Maybe. Maybe. Maybe.*

Maybe doing this thing is simply the wrong thing to do.

The work drudged on in the same manner as the day before. Yuri coded nonstop, rarely pausing for anything. Almonzo gushed at the pace and talent on display. Every facility had its own challenges. Whether an outdated interface engine or a proprietary one, it didn't matter. Yuri's systems impressed on that front as well by setting the stage for standardization to a level that never existed before. He could do no wrong, and the crowd of onlookers grew from Almonzo, to other engineers on their breaks, and even the four TerraFission engineers.

By the end of the day, Almonzo and Chelsea, of all people, helped Yuri finish the last ten sites. Would Yuri joke later about how the stupid Americans did his work for him? No, he wouldn't. He only pitied them and himself for how he would mourn them.

Bending over and covering his face in his hands, Yuri fought back tears for what he had done.

"Are you okay, my friend?" Almonzo asked.

Friend? Yuri sat up straight and forced a smile. "I'm sorry. This has been exhausting, but I think we're finished."

"Beers are on me," Almonzo said.

Exhaustion from the hurried work made it hard for Yuri to think; a fog swept over his brain. He glanced at his watch, noting that it had yet to turn three in the afternoon. *But there's something else I need to do. Something important. What? Beer would be nice . . . and not nice.* The taste of the beer that Gideon's neighbor had bought for him, well for Yuri technically, came to mind. "No IPAs," Yuri said.

"Of course not." Almonzo cringed. "Vile stuff. And since it's on me, only domestic. And by domestic, I mean Corona." Almonzo elbowed Yuri and chuckled.

You will be missed. Yuri smiled at Almanzo, giving into his charm. "Let's get some of this code into production." None of it mattered and nothing could be done for Project Ogon until Yuri left and triggered everything remotely.

"No." Almonzo stood up. "You've done enough today." He raised a hand toward Chelsea. "We all have. Let's grab a beer."

Chelsea stood in support. "I'm game."

I've won over my fiercest critic, from war to peace.

Chelsea smiled at Yuri. Long brunette hair rolled on top of the shoulders of her black, ribbed sweater. Bright red lipstick, outlined in dark lip liner contrasted with the black rims of her glasses. Her slight frame and triangular face matched Sasha's in such a way that Yuri wouldn't have doubted them sisters. Yuri squinted at Chelsea. *Is she in on it? I wonder if she's ever been to Sochi.* The good Doctor Sidorov always held contingencies within contingencies, plans within plans, wheels working inside of other wheels. Almonzo gained a squint as well. Was he also an agent of Mikel's?

"Don't worry about leaving early." Almonzo placed a hand on Yuri's shoulder. "I've certainly earned it, and nobody here believes outside consultants work a full day anyway."

Chelsea laughed. "You got that part right."

Almonzo pinched a frown at her, then laughed as well. "I knew it."

"All right." Yuri closed his laptop and stuffed it in his backpack. "Let's grab a beer, but I'm paying." He looked down and squeezed out familiar words. "I have an expense account." The same thing Gideon told Yuri when they first met. *Gideon you stupid, trusting, fool.*

After naming a nearby place, Chelsea left to gather whoever remained from TerraFission. Almonzo said that he'd only have a couple of drinks and that he would drive Yuri. When they left the control room, Almonzo didn't tell anyone else that he was leaving and peeked around corners as if he were sneaking out, even though he had said it wouldn't be a problem.

The excitement of getting away with something seemed extremely out of place considering that Yuri planned to destroy most of the East Coast and pockets of the rest of the continental United States of America. Yuri tilted his head. *And something else.*

At least he could compartmentalize these moments and set personal feelings aside. His affection toward Almanzo could be enjoyed while it lasted, but . . ..

Janna and Millie. Yuri stopped flat footed. How could he forget about them? *This program. The doctor's conditioning. It's too much.* Pulling out his phone, Yuri frantically searched for their location. Nothing had changed since the morning. *They're dead.* His stomach sank. Why hadn't he done something? What could he have done? It didn't make it any easier knowing that even he had been powerless to save them.

Yuri opened the message from the unknown phone. The numbers had kept coming but repeated in a series over and over.

"Let's get out of here." Almonzo's eyes darted around. "I don't want anyone stopping me with stupid questions."

Following Almonzo into the elevator, then outside and into the parking garage, Yuri stared at his phone, studying the numbers. What do they mean? He read them aloud, gaining a sideways glance from Almonzo. "42. 21. 199. 71. 4. 408. That's a geocache. Millie!"

Almonzo held out his car keys and stood next to a mid-size sedan. "What is it, Gideon?"

"My kid needs me. Can you take me into the city?" Yuri asked.

"And stand up TerraFission?" Almonzo shrugged. "Sure. Why not? I like the city and I can pick your brain some more on the way."

"Thank you," Yuri said, hurrying to the passenger door.

Tires screeched and an engine roared behind them. Yuri turned and had to jump back to avoid being hit by a pitch-black SUV. "Look out," Yuri yelled to Almanzo, but it was too late. The SUV plowed into Almanzo's car, launching it into the engineer.

Tires screeched again and the SUV pulled back, facing Yuri. The reinforced grill allowed maximum damage given and none taken. The driver's door flew open, and Dmitri hopped out. "Get in," he said.

No signs of movement came from the other side of the car.

"We can't leave him." Yuri gritted his teeth at Dmitri, then foolishly darted toward Almanzo.

"I won't ask again," Dmitri barked.

Yuri nodded, then entered the vehicle on the passenger front side. What did it matter? Almanzo would die tomorrow anyway. *I hope you passed quickly, my friend.*

Dmitri sent a message on his phone and immediately received a tone indicating a response. His face turned blank, and he pulled the SUV away. The man usually didn't say much and never lost a wink of sleep from any of the lives he'd taken. They drove for some time before Yuri calmed himself enough to speak. But, what to ask? Had Dmitri killed Janna and let Millie escape? Was it only wishful thinking that translated the numbers into geocache coordinates? He had to know.

"Did you eliminate the woman and her child?" Yuri asked as unemotionally as he could muster.

"No," Dmitri said, not offering anything else.

Infuriating. "Did Sasha?"

Dmitri huffed. "Not yet."

Yuri leaned his head back, hopeful, but frozen in place so as to not betray anything. "What does Mikel say about all this?"

Clenching his jaw, Dmitri grunted. He rolled his neck around; the bones within cracked loudly, filling the car cabin. "The doctor thinks it is only a matter of time, but Sasha thinks you need to act quickly in case he is wrong. If they talk to the right people and convince them to listen, then all is for nothing. Da?"

Dmitri glanced at Yuri, then back to the road. "Sasha says you told them everything. She hunts them. Says she'll gut them when she finds them and clean up your mess."

"I didn't tell them anything." Yuri gulped. "You have to believe me."

He laughed a low laugh. "Nobody ever asks Dmitri to think. They only tell him what to think. But I do think more than anyone knows. In this case, I do think. I think, 'Why would Yuri still do the work after telling his suka how to stop him?' I do not believe you betrayed us, as Sasha does, my friend." Dmitri attempted a smile at Yuri, but his lips only pulled away from his teeth in a grotesque display as if the man had never attempted a smile in his life. The failed gesture did nothing to reassure Yuri.

A message pinged Yuri's phone, "40."

"Is that the foolish American whore or the stupid, wide-eyed girl telling you where they are?"

The blood drained from Yuri's face. "No. Wrong number. Spam."

"Really?" Dmitri's focus left the road and trained fully on Yuri.

Yuri attempted to portray a calm, casual demeanor, but his nerves chewed at him from the inside. His face tightened, and he found himself unable to mutter a protest.

Dmitri's lip curled, resembling more of a smile than his forced one earlier. "And this is why they do not let Dmitri think. I told them you would never betray us."

"I didn't." Yuri said. He had no trouble saying that. *It's true. Isn't it?*

"You know what this means." Dmitri casually looked back at the road, but his fingers crunched the steering wheel, telling a more honest story.

"You can't kill me. You need me."

"We need your hands and eyeballs for the remote access. We don't need you."

Yuri lunged for the steering wheel. Dmitri's elbow met the side of his head.

Integration.

My face slammed against the side window of the car, and I slumped limply against the door. Sirens wailed in my ear, and the side of my face stung and burned with a fresh, bleeding wound. I let my head slide against the dashboard, and my left arm hang to my side, not wanting another strike from Dmitri.

"Are you out?" Dmitri asked. "Must have been lucky blow." He grabbed my shoulder and yanked me back.

I seized his thumb and wrist and attempted to wrench them around to disable him, but he didn't budge. Dmitri's strength went deeper than his muscles. He slammed on the brakes of the SUV, sending my head bouncing off the dash, tearing open more skin.

"Da. That is the Yuri I know." He put the car in park and went for my throat. I managed to get my hands between his thick fingers, two in each hand, and wrenched them apart, filling the cabin with stomach wrenching snaps and pops as they broke.

Dmitri screamed and pulled his mangled hand back into his jacket, reaching for his gun. I pivoted, and hit him hard with my elbow, twice, landing on his cheek and chin. It only slowed him. His pistol arched toward me, and I lunged for it, grabbing with both hands. The gun fired, deafening me. A silent scream poured from my lips, and I fought with all my strength to keep the gun away. My grip slipped as blood seeped from his broken skin, bone protruding through knuckles.

The gun went off twice more. Bullets grazed my temple. Dmitri wrenched the steering wheel with his other hand. His leverage pushed the pistol closer to my face. I tilted my head, then jerked it forward, biting an already torn finger. He screamed and dropped the gun—finally giving into pain.

The Russian seized my neck with both of his mangled hands. I couldn't breathe, and the immense pressure threatened to burst my ears and pop my eyes out of my skull before I died.

I scrambled, flailing my hands about, trying to get hold of anything to stop him. Dmitri grunted and pressed me down under his weight. I found something metal and squeezed it tightly. Then . . . his grip loosened.

I fired the gun again and again until it didn't recoil and then a few more times to make sure. I tossed the gun on the car floor. This man had been a comrade to Yuri, closer than what he had imagined a brother would be. He didn't mean anything to me, but I held Yuri's memories. The man had murdered indiscriminately and had just about killed me. Whether he did it for his country or if he did it because he liked to didn't matter anymore. His life, and the suffering that his life wrought had ended. I ended it.

Whoever *I* was. *Not Gideon. Not Yuri.*

I searched Dmitri's body. There wasn't as much blood as I expected. His heart must have stopped quickly. I pulled two extra magazines from his jacket and his phone from the left pocket. Protected by his massive body, the phone screen only had a single crack on it, possibly incurred from before our fight by the hefty bear claws he called hands. The phone indicated he had messages but wouldn't reveal them until unlocked.

Dmitri slumped; his head bowed. I grabbed his hair and lifted his gigantic melon of a head. Positioning the phone in front of his face unlocked the device *just as the designers intended*. Four recent messages from Sasha, only two unread. The two that Dmitri had read were bad news for Yuri.

"Good. With his work completed, finish him. He's not Yuri anymore, inside or out. Doctor confirmed he isn't needed."

Then, a minute later as if an afterthought. "Don't forget his hands and eyes are needed to unlock the biometric."

I lowered Dmitri's phone. My breathing wavered. *These sick animals. Who would do something like that?* Yuri would have done that. I curled my nose, pushing back the memories of the things Yuri had done. I wiped a tear away from my cheek that hadn't warned me of its arrival, a tear for *Gideon.*

Yuri had held the gun in front of him, with barely any expression on his face or inflection in his voice when he told Gideon that he had everything he needed and that he didn't need Gideon anymore. *These people.* The way they discarded people like garbage once they had used them up.

I held my palms in front of my face. Where was the blood? Dmitri's blood, Gideon's blood? My hearing had begun its journey back and had taken the form of a maddening high-pitched wail. Gideon's face, bruised and bloody, with no tears, and empty, already dead eyes, stared through me. The gun before me, the wailing in my ears screaming for Yuri to stop, but he didn't. *I didn't.*

The gun on the floor of Dmitri's car called for me to pick it up and avenge Gideon by taking his murderer's life. I lived in Yuri's body. I had Yuri's memories, but I didn't have any idea how Yuri thought or felt. His memories only played in my mind like old film. I could infer emotion, but the images of Yuri's mother, of Sasha, even of his childhood dog Dymchato, *Smokey*, brought nothing to my heart.

While Yuri's life dominated my brain, my face and fingerprints belonged to Gideon and painfully, tragically, my heart belonged to Janna and Millie. *I'm going to keep on living. I live for them.*

How long will *I* be in control? Will Yuri come back? Even if he does, there would be no going back to the Russians now. At least he could keep Janna and Millie safe.

A car honked behind me, then sped around the outside of the car. The angry person inside shook a fist at Dmitri as he went by. I shook my head, then sighed at the prospect of dragging Dmitri into the back of the SUV. Even with the casual traffic, I needed to get the car off the road.

Dmitri's phone had locked once more, so I held it up to his face again. I then changed his settings to not lock his phone anymore, again, *not exactly as secure as the designers intended.* I read the two unread messages from Sasha.

"Meeting soon with Gideon's family."

"Report in when you are finished."

I believed Millie had given me coordinates, but Sasha may have found them another way or deciphered the message. I needed to know what she knew. I searched Yuri's memory. They didn't code their messages with anything as simple as a poly cipher. These messages were direct, just avoiding words that would put them on an automatic government list.

"Finished with Yuri. Where should we meet?" I sent Sasha from Dmitri's phone.

I couldn't drag Dmitri into the back seat in one attempt. The effort required me to exit the vehicle, push him partway, pull more of him from the back seat, and pry him up at times. Yuri's dead friend did not cooperate, so, out of breath, I settled for leaving him face down behind the passenger seat with one leg spread across the back seats. *Good enough.* The tinted windows hid most of my horrible deed but failed to protect me from the occasional honk of a car horn and at least two obscene gestures.

No reply from Sasha. I punched in the coordinates into the geocache app, "N 42° 21.199' W 71° 4.408'" It brought up a location, Commonwealth Avenue in downtown Boston, a wooded area. *Thank God. Millie and Janna, I'm coming for you.*

With no time to lose, and at least a twenty-minute drive, I drove as fast as I dared without drawing attention. *If Sasha has them already . . ..* The idea nearly emptied my stomach.

Time dragged during the trip while I alternated between beating the steering wheel, looking at Dmitri's phone, and looking at the map on my phone. I searched my mind for answers. *I did warn them. I did tell them everything.*

I searched Yuri's memories, everything yielded, how to find people, how to follow without being seen, how to hack phones and pull information from all of the ride sharing and house rental applications that had made modern lives that much easier. Yuri had all these memories, and so did I, but they weren't there because he had been trained to save people. He had been trained to kill them, with every weapon imaginable or even his bare hands. The memory of Gideon's death sickened me again.

"No. I need something useful, Yuri. Give me something that can help me find them." I beat the steering wheel some more. How did they get away? Had Yuri helped them somehow? A memory flashed over me, but this memory belonged to *me*.

* * *

"Wake up, Janna. I need you to listen." I shook Janna from her sleep.

Janna smiled her beautiful half smile, and said hoarsely, "What is it?"

I sat on the bed and grabbed her shoulder tightly, unable to think of what to say, but there wasn't enough time to think. "I'm not your husband," I blurted out.

"Shut up." She closed her eyes. "Weirdo."

"You need to listen."

Her face paled enough to notice in the dark. "You're scaring me."

"Good. You're in danger."

Janna sat up and pulled away, wrapping her arms around her knees, tears already forming. "What are you talking about?" Janna croaked with a sniff.

"I don't know how much time there is, so I can't tell you everything, but I have to tell you." A knot formed in my throat, attempting to stop me from confessing. "Gideon didn't return from captivity. He was killed over there."

Her cries burned my soul.

"I was the one that did it. I killed your husband and—"

Springing off the bed, Jena threw her hands up. "Are you crazy? Just leave if you don't want to be here. Don't come at me with some crazy story."

I stood and grabbed her by the wrists. "You need to get your things, get Millie, and use the credit cards to get as much money as possible. There are people in . . . that will come for you; they're in the hotel."

Janna's mouth gaped open in a jagged frown. Tears ran down her face. "Stop it," she pleaded. "I knew this was all too good to be true."

"It's going to be bad. They are going to attack . . .." I grabbed my head as searing pain stabbed my brain. "It's the power plants. We're going to attack them all. It's why we're here."

"Who is *we*? You aren't making sense. You're a software guy." Janna laughed uneasily. "Are you drunk?"

"Get the cash." I pulled out my wallet and gave it to her. "Don't use the cards anywhere else after getting as much money as you can. Start in the lobby."

Janna's face flushed; her brow lowered.

"You can't leave town until tomorrow, but you have to leave the hotel. Don't go anywhere near a bus, train, or plane. Even a ride share will show a pattern if you try to leave town."

Digging her fingers into my arm, Janna shook me. "This is mad. Why are you saying this?" She looked down the hall. "Millie."

She dug her nails in deeper. "Who's *we* Gideon? I was told to keep an . . . Agent Spencer . . .. What have you gotten us into?"

"Menya zovut Yuri Volkov. Tebe nuzhno uyti." I stared at Janna coldly. The pain in my head returned, stronger.

Putting both her hands up, Janna backed away, her eyes shot wide with realization.

I grabbed my head, not stopping the pain, and closed my eyes. "Call the police, the FBI, Homeland Security if you want, but I fear that you'll end up dead if you do. We have ears everywhere. Get the cash. Run and hide. Find somewhere to stay. Pay in cash, but leave the city, all cities, tomorrow morning, western Connecticut or upstate New York would be good."

"Everywhere needs a credit card for deposit. We can't run. I won't know what I'm doing." Janna bit her fist and looked away.

"After tonight, you can use them again. But today pay them extra cash if you need to. Tell them you're hiding from your husband." The pain tripled and I fell to my knees. "You're smart. You can do this, but you have to go. Go now!"

"Millie will never understand." Janna stepped toward me and spat as she talked. "She'll hate me for this and never forgive me."

"It's better than being dead," I struggled out. "They did something to me, and I'm going to not remember this talk, I think." I laughed.

Janna groaned.

"But he loves you too, both of you. So, I trust him to do the right thing. He'll find a way to save you. He has to. Just give him enough time."

"You're insane, Gideon."

* * *

"You don't want to be Yuri anymore, do you?" I squeezed the steering wheel, giving it a reprieve from the beatings. "What do we do?" At least Yuri didn't answer me. *You're only insane if the voices in your head answer you. True.*

My top priority had to be ensuring Janna's and Millie's survival. Yuri's memories contained details on how to hide and how to move without notice, but I had to do more than save the girls. I tried to convince myself that Project Ogon couldn't proceed without me, but Doctor Sidorov, and his team in Sochi, would find a way to continue. They simply knew too much about the systems now and everything had been placed in position. How could I stop them?

Surely, I'd seen Mr. Spencer twice at the hotel, posing as a kid in a hoodie of all things. My eyebrows came together. *Maybe he wasn't trying to look like a kid. Maybe he's just young.* Could I trust Mr. Spencer, Agent Spencer, though? He may have been part of Mikel's plans. Maybe I could go to the press. The only reporter I knew, Claude, had likely gone back to Switzerland. *No. By the time the press got to work, Janna and Millie would be . . . I should capture Mr. Spencer, find out what he knows, and make him bring in the Americans to stop it all.*

No, Yuri could do all those things because his heart was in it. If I tried, I'd make a mistake and end up dead or kill Agent Spencer, and I didn't know if the latter was a good thing or not. Every plan I could think of required too much time to complete.

I shook my head and pulled along Commonwealth Avenue, closing in on the location Millie had sent me. Still late afternoon, the sun had not started to set, and people walked in every direction. Neither Janna nor Millie seemed to be among them.

Parking the car on Berkley, I grabbed Dmitri's gun and stuffed it in the back of my pants and untucked my shirt to hide it. I jumped out and locked the doors, sparing a glance at Dmitri's hulking shadow through the tinted windows. If someone looked in, they'd think of him as laundry or something, a lot of laundry. *Hopefully.*

My phone guided me to the exact spot Millie had sent. I frantically searched around for her and Janna, but neither were around. *Stupid. They wouldn't hang out in the open all day.* I scrutinized the area more closely. Large trees canopied the entire section, providing a park experience for the central walkway that ran through the area. A lot of people used the passage as a pleasant walking path to get where they were going, while others had come to simply enjoy nature by sitting on benches or on the grass in groups.

A lone statue stood nearby. *Very geocachey.* I walked up to it, providing its only attendance. A depiction of Alexander Hamilton looked past me, one hand on his chest, and one foot stepping forward. I traced the direction his foot pointed and came to a large tree. I followed that path and searched the ground around the large base. I could find nothing out of the ordinary, even under a raised, gnarled root.

I sighed and searched up the trunk and through the branches, thick with leaves that had begun their change into a beautiful autumnal reddish-brown. Again, nothing showed, and really nothing within Janna or Millie's reach. I traced the branches to their source, three large boughs that twisted out of the trunk where I finally noticed the corner of a small cardboard box resting mostly out of site.

The geocache application did not register the cache as official. *Definitely Millie.* I grabbed the box. Small, paperboard, and probably made to store a sandwich for a day, the box did not resemble your typical geocache box. I opened it and revealed only a small, scribbled note.

"28 Zneyobebhtu."

Another puzzle and another reason to believe Millie had given me these clues. This clue, though, brought my horrible joke about Polish names to mind. *Pawel. Is he okay?* Or was he also part of Sidorov's schemes? Sidorov always said things like, "I had planned for that." When on the same team, I easily dismissed these statements, believing that he said things like that when something unexpected happened. With how close Mikel had come to destroying America and possibly still could, maybe he *had* planned for everything. Maybe he had planned for Yuri to literally lose his mind. Maybe he had planned for me. Maybe Chelsea was my backup and had already set things in motion. Just like the chess game we played, Sidorov sacrificed valuable pieces on the board like Dmitri and me. Mikel made plans, and I only had "maybes."

My Internet searches revealed nothing when looking for Zneyobebhtu. I balled up the note and put it in my pocket, then placed the box back in the tree. If Millie came back, she would know I had received her message.

I walked back to the statue and tilted my head up, eyeballing Mr. Hamilton. "Do you have any ideas?" I asked the first Treasurer of the United States of America. He didn't offer any help.

Bringing up my settings on my phone, I unblocked my hidden applications given to me by the Sochi team, well, Yuri's hidden applications. My hand shook as I typed the information in, both hoping I found nothing and hoping that I'd find something and be the only one who did. If anything turned up on these applications, then Sasha would surely have them. Is that what she meant by, "Meeting soon with Gideon's family?"

Nothing turned up for phone tracking, credit cards, currency transfer apps, or any travel accounts. *Good job, Janna.* I accessed the deeper network data-exchange that had been granted to those of us in Project Ogon. I found the fresh kill order for me, placed by Sasha. *Great.* She must not have believed me dead or the text that *Dmitri* had sent her. I searched deeper, finding the alert, a capture not kill order, for Janna and Millie. Nothing had turned up on facial recognition at any travel hubs or online street cams. They'd been cautious or lucky. But . . . why did I still have access to all of this from my phone if they had put the order in for my death?

I growled and hurled my phone away from me as far as I could. *Yuri would never be so careless. They're tracking you, tracking your searches to find them.* My access and data had likely been limited to searches about my family so that I would lead them right to Janna and Millie. *They're tracking Dmitri's phone also.*

I pulled out Dmitri's phone, ready to chuck it as well, but hesitated. *What had he been tracking?* I opened up his tracking app. Only two entries. Yuri's phone about sixty meters away . . . and Sasha's less than a mile away.

Resolution.

Drilling down on Sasha's location yielded me both comfort and anxiety. The lunatic likely wasn't hiding in a tree with a rifle trained on me. She lingered on Berkley, where I left the car, and Dmitri's body. At least her phone did. I scanned the trees. None offered a good line of sight conducive to a sniper, but the perspective line of sight for a target often seemed vastly different for a shooter. I glanced down at Dmitri's phone. Sasha's location had disappeared from the application. Shaking the phone in an ignorant display, I tried to bring it back. She masked her location. Why hadn't I thought of that? Why hadn't Yuri's memories told me that? I supposed that they inconveniently provided answers to only questions I asked.

"Do you really think you'll find them before me, Yuri?" Sasha's message popped up on Dmitri's phone.

Crap. I hurled Dmitri's phone over the trees gaining a quizzical look from a short, stout woman walking her dog. Why did I do that? Running in the direction opposite Sasha without thinking, I racked my brain about the cryptic message Millie left for me. *Cryptic. Of course!*

The geocaching community wanted people to have a fun challenge, but they also wanted players to have success. The coordinates provided a rough location of the cache, but not the exact point. Participants had to find it, and sometimes they were well hidden. Therefore, hints were often supplied to make things easier. The hints were cyphered using a simple key.

```
A|B|C|D|E|F|G|H|I|J|K|L|M
-------------------------
N|O|P|Q|R|S|T|U|V|W|X|Y|Z
```

I pulled out Millie's note. "28 Zneyobebhtu." *It's an address. Z to M. N to A. E to R. Marlborough. 28 Marlborough.*

Reaching for my phone . . . *crap.* I instead grabbed a man walking by on the busy sidewalk. He reeled back when I screamed at him. "Marlborough. Where's Marlborough?"

He pointed and stammered. "T-two blocks up."

The man broke free of my grip then scrambled away. "Town's crazier every day."

Heart filling with hope, I sprinted in the direction he had pointed. Several cars honked as I crossed the street, but I didn't slow. I patted under the back of my shirt, checking that Dmitri's gun remained. I'd need it to stop Sasha.

I darted around people on the busy sidewalks and through the roads packed with cars until I reached Marlborough. The street didn't have residences on it, only businesses-like storage warehouses. I ran and stopped at the front of each building, frustrated that none held the address of twenty-eight. I pulled out Millie's message again. Is it a reverse key? My panic prevented me from effectively reversing it. *Why? This has to be it. You have to find them; you simply have no choice. Surrender.*

I crumpled the paper note and stared past the buildings, trying my best not to think of Sasha doing the horrible things from Yuri's memories to my wife and daughter, to *Gideon's* wife and daughter. The structures behind the warehouses had flat facades, and sparse windows, some with draperies typical to—*residential.*

I hurried between the warehouses into a large alleyway connecting named streets, where what I had seen revealed itself to be the rear of five or six brownstones that hugged each other closely, the address closest to me being twenty-two. The tall apartment buildings behind me to the southwest blocked the sunlight, casting shadows from the early evening sun. I could spot address number twenty-eight from where I stood.

Thankfully, no black SUVs parked nearby. Each of the four-story brownstones had bricks of a different color, red, brown, yellow, tan. I could never have lived with Janna and Millie in something like these. We needed our space. I shook my head. *I've never really lived anywhere with them. Get them safe, then think of the future.*

I couldn't just walk up to the door and knock. Sasha could be there already. Someone had left the top window of Twenty-Eight Marlborough Street cracked open, possibly a bathroom. A gutter ran up between the window and the brownstone next to it. *Can I scramble up that thing?* It wouldn't support my weight on its own. I racked my brain for similar experiences. *Yes. Yuri can do this.*

I took off my shoes and socks. I'd need the surface tension against the bricks to scurry up using the gutter for help. I scanned the windows and the alley for onlookers. Seeing none, I seized the moment and ran for the gutter. Unsure at first, muscle memory kicked in, and I had the window open in no time, sliding inside the building, and closing the window behind me. I locked it ensuring Sasha wouldn't be getting in that way.

Inside my head, I laughed. What would I have done if someone was using this bathroom? I stepped for the door. The old brownstone's floors creaked underneath each step. I stopped, then carefully crept closer to the vanity, stepping on places more likely to be reinforced or used to heavier weight. The floor still complained, but faintly. I cracked open the door. Seeing nobody in the hallway, I ventured out of the bathroom.

Black and white portraits of what I could assume were relations of the home's owners interrupted the maroon and white vertically striped pattern on the wallpapered hall. Continuing my stealth, and sticking to the walls, I checked the two bedrooms for Janna and Millie with no success.

My, although cautious, trip down the stairs to the third floor announced my coming to anyone who listened. My inspection of the two bedrooms on this floor revealed Janna's and Millie's roller bags in the larger of the two rooms, and thankfully, no strangers. A loud thump, followed by abrupt high-pitch voices traveled up the stairs announcing activity below. I turned and headed for the stairwell. No more noise and no people revealed themselves.

The second floor contained an unpopulated family room with a smallish television for the times, a faded orange sofa, and an old blue reclining chair. The wallpaper had begun to yellow with age, fading the pattern, a fleur-de-lis or something. In spite of my urgency, I scrunched my nose at the hideously decorated room.

The other room turned out to be a dining room, with a table set for three people, but no one there either. That left the now silent ground floor. *Please be okay. Sasha could be keeping them alive to use them to force me back into Sidorov's mission, to trigger the reactions remotely. I still had value—my hands and eyeballs at least.*

As I snuck down the spiral staircase to the first floor, Janna's profile revealed itself to me sitting in a lounge chair, straight as a rail, tears on her cheeks. My stomach sank . . . the unforgivable pain I had caused. Two more steps revealed Millie. Her tear-soaked eyes darted up to me, but she minutely shook her head. I froze.

"Were you trying to be quiet, my love?" Sasha asked.

Dammit. I removed Dmitri's gun and raised it eye level, taking the remaining stairs quickly and training the gun on Sasha.

She lazily lounged in her chair, dressed all in black, pants, shirt, boots, jacket, casually pointing her gun, with an extended barrel, a silencer, at Millie. "Is that Dmitri's gun? He wouldn't want it pointed at me."

The main three women in my fresh new life sat in spacious lounge chairs, surrounded by bookshelves around a coffee table in the cozy den, just off the front door. The place must have taken a lifetime for the owners to fill with books, knickknacks, quaint pictures on the walls, a large Fleur de Lis jar on the end table between Janna and Millie, and a pile of coffee table books on the table between Millie and Sasha. The entire decor could have fit well in a Sherlock Holmes novel, minus a fireplace.

"It's over Sasha. The doctor wouldn't want you exposing yourself like this. Why are you here?" I didn't lower my gun. The things she'd done in front of Yuri, the things he'd heard of her doing, creative torture and callous murders, all the while enjoying herself, chilled me to the bone. She famously often flouted command and did what she wanted to satisfy the cruel demons within her. Maybe I could exploit that, distract her, make her sloppy. "Are you going off mission again?"

"Gideon . . . please," Janna said softly.

"Not Gideon," Sasha bit back.

It was only then that I noticed the woman lying by the front door, in a pool of blood. Gray, short cut curled hair now stuck to her head, and her round cheeks on her round face. A baggy sweater soaked up what it could. The woman would have painted a friendly picture as greeter to this bed and breakfast. Instead, she lay there as the unfortunate collateral damage, one of hundreds, that always added to the cost of engaging Sasha or Dmitri or, as I recalled, Yuri.

"Why would you pick these simple cows over me, my love?" Sasha asked.

I should just shoot her and pray for the best. I regarded Sasha. Reckless as usual, she took too much risk. *I'll end this now.* But with Sasha aiming her gun at Millie, she could accidentally shoot Millie if it went off, and I could put Millie in more danger than she already faced.

"Stand up," Sasha said to Millie.

Millie stood, now sobbing and looking at the floor.

"No," Janna sprang out of her chair, grabbing my attention, but not Sasha's. Sasha still looked at my daughter. *Gideon's daughter.*

"Fine." Sasha giggled. "Janna. Take the gun from *Yuri* and set it on this table. Don't be stupid about it and end up getting your daughter killed." Sasha motioned to Millie with the gun.

Janna turned and stepped toward me.

"Wait." I held one hand toward Janna. "I'm not going to play one of your mind games Sasha. How can I fix this? What's your endgame? What do you want?"

"What I've always wanted," Sasha mumbled, sounding distant.

So, she could possibly be reasoned with. "I give you what you want, and you'll leave them alone."

"Yes." Sasha stood, tears in her eyes. "Yes, lover, give me what I want, and I will not harm them." Her face softened, but her grip did not. The gun inched closer to Millie, increasing Millie's sobbing.

"Okay. I'll do anything you want." I handed the gun to Janna, who quickly sat it on the table and rushed to Millie's side.

Sasha lowered her gun and looked at Millie. "GPS coordinates? Really? Idiot girl, we would have found you without his help." Sasha jerked her head toward me.

I gritted my teeth. *Do not talk to Millie that way.*

"But tracking our asset proved just as simple." Sasha pointed her gun at Janna and smiled.

"No, you promised." I inched forward.

Sasha sighed. "I did promise you, my love."

I raised my voice. "Tell me what you want."

"How I'd love to torture and kill them in front of you. That is one thing I want, but who knows if you'd ever come back to me after that." She lowered the gun again and looked at me, grinning. "I want what I've always wanted. I want you."

Me. I don't exist.

"Take him then. Leave us alone," Janna said.

"Be silent, cow." Sasha reared the gun back to strike Janna, who raised her chin defiantly.

Sasha made a fist with her other hand and screamed. She turned and kicked over the coffee table, flipping Dmitri's gun against a bookcase. Straightening her jacket, Sasha smiled tightly at me and pointed her gun back at Millie. "See. I do not harm."

I pinched my brow tightly and looked at Janna, her face pale and frowning. Millie faced the ground, still huffing and sobbing. *Fine. Give into Sasha. Get her to lower her guard and disable her, even if I have to die trying.* "I'm yours."

Janna shook her head and wrapped an arm around Millie. Would the pain I caused them ever end?

"I know you better than the doctor says you know yourself, Yuri." She swept her gun at Janna and Millie. "These girls are all you want in this world right now." She pointed the gun at my head. "The doctor put those thoughts in your head. If you leave with me right now, you'll do something stupid and get yourself killed, possibly even kill me in the process." She pointed her gun toward the bookcases.

My eyes darted to Dmitri's gun on the floor behind Sasha. *She's right. I do want to do something stupid.*

"But you know we are everywhere. If you are anything less than cooperative, these women will die, even if not by my hand."

"After tomorrow, it won't matter if *we* kill them. This entire city will be sick with radiation; they'll be the walking dead," I said.

"Assuming you finish the job. Yes. Not bomb." Sasha's lips curled into a cruel smile as she mocked Mikel's words. "How did you say that? Killing two birds."

Millie laughed a shocked giggle between sobs, pulling a confused, angry glance from Sasha.

Waving her gun at the door, Sasha frowned. "There is nothing more to say, nothing more to do. The doctor will put you back together. He promised me he would bring my Yuri back."

But Yuri doesn't want to come back. I sucked in a deep breath and stole one last look at Janna and Millie. Even in their dire straits, I would never see anything more beautiful than them. *I can still save them.*

"Now you can get out of town as fast as you can. Use the cards. None of that matters now," I said to them.

Millie met my eyes and nodded. Janna only locked eyes on Millie and hugged her.

I hurried past them toward the door.

Sasha's steps followed but stopped at Janna and Millie. "Fine. But give me your phones and do not leave here for at least two hours. That will give us time to finish Yuri's work. You'll be watched."

Janna and Millie reluctantly handed Sasha their phones.

Sasha snapped both in half and tossed them aside. She smiled at me and closed the distance between us, placing a hand on my cheek and her gun at my side. "Part of you will remember how kind I can be, how I make sacrifices for you. You will come back to me, my love."

I guiltily looked over Sasha's shoulder toward Gideon's family. The words likely didn't burn Janna anymore, but they did me. I'd never be Sasha's again no matter how much Sasha longed for it. Sidorov would likely fail with me or create some other darker version of me, but Sasha's Yuri had likely perished soon after Gideon had. Whatever lie he had told Sasha would reveal itself over time. I pitied her for the suffering that she had likely endured watching her *lover* be broken and twisted, only for him to fall in love with another woman. The doctor would break Sasha's heart all over again.

At least Janna and Millie had a chance. At least I'd given them that.

A flash of gold, followed by a crash, as loud as a gunshot, sent Sasha to the ground. I spun around, defensively.

"Turn your back on me, bitch." Janna hovered over our tormentor. The Fleur de Lis jar lay broken in pieces all around Sasha.

I wrestled Sasha's gun from her weak hand.

She moaned. "No." Sasha pushed herself up, then collapsed on the floor.

I handed the gun to Janna. She considered it, wide-eyed, then accepted it.

"I lov—" My face reddened.

So did Janna's. She turned her attention to Sasha.

I wanted to tell her how much I loved her, but none of that could happen now.

"Dad." Millie said, pained.

"Everything's going to be fine," I told her.

"Is it?" Janna stepped back, half raising the gun that I'd just given her, possibly in error, toward me.

I held out a hand in defense. My body ached, especially my side. I fought back tears, rolling my lips into a flat line, holding back any emotion. Was there any way I could have a life with them in it?

Millie's face paled. She gaped and reached to my side. "You've been shot!"

Snapping my chin down confirmed Millie's assessment, a hole and a growing spot of red on my white dress shirt. Sasha must have fired when Janna struck her. "It's nothing," I said. Whether it was movie memories or Yuri memories telling me that, I didn't really know. The increasingly sharp pain from the wound said otherwise. I stumbled toward a chair and leaned against the back of it with Janna and Millie's help.

I pointed at the front door where a new bullet hole splintered the frame. "In and out. I think that's always good."

"We have to get you to a hospital," Millie said. She scrambled to the floor before the bookcase and awkwardly picked up Dmitri's gun, inspecting it starry-eyed.

"Give me that." Janna snatched the gun from Millie and stuffed it into the back of her jeans like I had. She pressed a couch blanket against the front and back of my wound, applying pressure. She didn't meet my eyes. "What do you expect us all to do now? If what Sasha said is true, we need to think about things carefully."

"I agree." The hair on the back of my neck tingled. Far from intimate, this could have been the last time Janna touched me.

"I'm going to call Ben," Janna said.

"Ben?" I asked.

Janna motioned to Millie, who took over applying pressure to my wound. Janna produced a business card from her rear, pants pocket. "Agent Spencer. I should have called him when you started acting weird, but you really spooked me."

Mr. Spencer. "How do you know you can trust him?"

"I can't, can I?" Janna frowned. "He approached us after you left from coffee the other day. He asked about odd behavior and strange associates. He brought up that reporter, Claude. I called the field office and talked to his boss. At least he *does* work for the FBI."

"Then he's more ours than yours," Sasha groaned, pushing herself to her knees and wiping blood from her ear and nose.

Janna spun around on her feet, pointing Sasha's gun at her. "Give me your phone, or . . .."

"Or what?" Sasha stood, wobbly, but trained a confident glare at Janna. "Nothing has changed, except that now it will take everything I have not to kill you and your mewling daughter. That is, if Yuri leaves with me and I don't change my mind because of your outburst. Maybe I just kill one of you."

"Give me a gun, Janna," I said.

Janna stepped back but didn't hand me either gun.

Sasha's eyes filled with tears, and her tiny lips scrunched together. "And you'd kill me, wouldn't you, lover?"

Without hesitation. The memories I had of her would haunt me for the rest of my days.

A tear fell down Sasha's cheek. "It would have been you and me against the world, my love. But, I suppose, now you all die."

Sasha pulled a knife from her jacket. One of many that Yuri had memory of. *Crap. These memories are not timely.* She held it at her side, glancing at Janna who held steady, pointing the gun at Sasha. Flipping the knife up, Sasha caught it by the blade, and launched it at me. In such close quarters, I reacted, stopping it with my forearm, avoiding a fatal blow.

Janna fired the gun and missed the leaping Sasha. The reduced recoil bobbled the gun in Janna's hands. Sasha knocked Janna down with a kick to the chest, sending the gun flying, then turned on me with another knife. Millie grabbed Sasha's hair and pulled back. Sasha elbowed Millie in the face, sending her over the chair behind her, then spun all the way around slicing at my neck with her blade, stinging as the tip of her blade nicked me.

Sasha grinned and assumed a fighting posture. "I almost had you."

I pulled the knife from my forearm, ready to take her on. Sasha would feign high but go low. Her blade work always set up her footwork. I'd have to avoid her strong kicks if I were to survive, assuming I had enough speed and energy to keep up with her. The fight with Dmitri and the wounds Sasha had given me were taking their toll.

The smile left Sasha's face, and her eyes shifted to my right. "You won't do it. You would have already."

Janna held Dmitri's gun and worked herself to her feet. "I'm going to. I'm just not very good at it." The gun shook in Janna's hands, but her finger remained steady on the trigger.

"No. I don't think so. You're not a—"

Janna shot Sasha in the chest and proceeded to shoot again and again after she fell back against the bookshelf until the pistol only clicked. We had that tendency in common, as well. *We would make a good team.* My ears rang, still not fully recovered from the first time they had endured the report of that gun this day.

I hobbled to Sasha and placed my hand on her neck and grabbed her wrist. She didn't have a pulse. I closed Sasha's eyes for the last time. I didn't like Sasha, and I certainly didn't love her, but Yuri had expressed his love to her a million times. Sasha loved Yuri so much that she died trying to bring him back. At least that part of their story pained my heart. Somehow, "I'm sorry," wouldn't cut it, so I didn't say anything. What could I say? I hovered in a cold, dead silence.

"Her phone," Janna said.

I rummaged through Sasha's jacket. Among a lot more knives, a slender wallet, and a pack of Dirol gum, I found her phone. Her face didn't unlock the device, but Yuri knew the passcode. The whole ordeal tore at my gut more than my bullet wound. Even Sasha didn't deserve the life she had been forced into or what eventually happened to her, but she sure put herself at risk. I couldn't tell if I was sad for her dying or if I was sad that not even I would mourn her properly.

"Mrs. Hernandez," Millie said.

I glanced at the poor woman who lay by the door, whom I knew nothing about. Speaking of not deserving what happened to them, Mrs. Hernandez deserved being murdered less than Sasha, if I could measure such an absurd thing.

I tossed the phone to Janna, who caught it in one hand, while the other hand pointed the gun at me.

"It's out of bullets," I said.

"Right." Janna scrunched her brows, then tossed Dmitri's gun onto a chair cushion.

I sighed in relief.

Janna picked Sasha's gun off the floor and trained it on me.

I shook my head and applied pressure to my side.

She called Agent Spencer, Agent "Ben" Spencer to be precise. I slumped next to Sasha and held my bullet wound.

Millie crouched next to me, wiping away her look of repulsion toward Sasha.

"Get away from him," Janna said, pointing the gun away from us.

"I'm fine," Millie said.

Janna explained things to Ben over the phone.

"I'm not an idiot," Millie said.

"I know." I grabbed her shoulder. "Why would you say that?"

Looking down, Millie lowered her voice. "That woman said I was stupid for giving you the GPS coordinates."

"Oh yeah, that."

"But that wasn't enough to find us, was it?" Millie asked.

"It wasn't." I chuckled. They would have had to find the statue and the box and decipher the message and assume it came from Janna or Millie. "You're lucky I was able to figure it out."

"Not really." Millie frowned. "Mom told me not to do it, but I didn't think you'd be careless enough to lead them here, Dad."

"I'm not your—"

"I know." Millie looked away. "Mom and I have been arguing about what you are."

"He's sending regular police," Janna said. "Ben said that even if we can't trust them, at least it's all on the radio and that will keep us alive until his people get here."

"I guess that will do. What did he say about the plot against America?"

"He . . . he seemed shocked but said he knew something was going on. He just thought you were stealing secrets. He's going to have every nuclear facility physically sever remote access immediately, and they are pulling something else down as well. I didn't understand it. When he gets here, you can tell him what to do."

"That should help, in case they found another way in. Give me her phone," I said to Janna.

She lowered her brows, then handed it to me. "Why?"

"I need to move them along; in case they still think they can win."

I searched through Sasha's contacts until I found Mikel.

"Hello," he said in English with his thick Sochi accent that he hadn't improved at all.

"It's over," I said.

Only breathing replied.

"The FBI has been alerted. They're locking you out and heading your way." I covered the receiver. "You told the FBI they were in the hotel, right?"

Janna shook her head.

Oh well. "I've stopped it all, and if they don't catch you, I will."

After a pause, Doctor Sidorov sighed into the receiver. "Yes. Yes. I planned for all of this." He ended the call.

Recourse.

I sat on the floor near where Sasha had fallen, the girls standing over me, while police and presumably agents or detectives scrambled around inside and outside the house. Two paramedics inspected and patched me up. Others had removed Sasha and Mrs. Hernandez, while the two working on me recommended that I go to the hospital instead of receiving field treatment. The youngest of them said he thought I'd probably be fine either way before his partner told him he didn't know what he was talking about. I believed the younger one.

Despite rushing from the hotel before four a.m. with no shower or makeup, Janna radiated with beauty. She nervously pulled on her clothes and bit her lip awkwardly listening to the many conversations around us. My lips parted and I looked at her wide eyed in amazement.

Her eyes met mine. "What?"

"I can't believe you did all this. Your escape, surviving an encounter with a Russian assassin, it's like you were born for this kind of work." I cringed as the paramedic pulled the tape off my back bandage and applied a new one.

"We barely survived." She curled her nose at me. "We grabbed the money like you said, then walked frantically, randomly for what seemed like an hour, but it only took minutes." Janna licked her lips. "Millie got out her phone and said we needed to ditch them, even though we had them in airplane mode. She tapped into the city's free Wi-Fi and got us a map to a coffee shop. We shoved the phones in a mailbox, argued over coffee, got a cab to the library, argued and researched some more, and found this b&b."

"What were you guys going to do next before I messed everything up?"

"We bought the burner phone. Mom wanted to contact someone for help. *I* wanted to get in touch with you, but Mom thought that was a bad idea," Millie said.

"Wasn't it?" Janna asked.

"Well, the plan wasn't bad . . . Dad, er, he messed it up somewhere along the way."

I beamed at Millie. She gave me hope.

"Initially, I wanted to call Agent Spencer, but I was reluctant because you scared the heck out of me, waking me up like that." Janna grabbed her elbow and let the other arm dangle. "We have some things to talk about."

I nodded. She meant that we needed to talk about *what* I was more than *who* I was. Or, what I'd done. Pretending to be her husband. Killing her husband. Where would I even start? My stomach sank with how badly I wanted to be with *my* family and how impossible that scenario would be.

"Was that woman right? Do you really think they can get to us no matter where we are, even protected by the FBI?" Janna asked, possibly changing the subject, possibly bringing up what she wanted to talk about.

"Yeah. I bet they're tracking *me* with some sort of device, as well." I ran my tongue across the front of my teeth. "Probably one in a tooth, or a tracker injection, or a real implant, the best ones are really big. Yuri must have been unconscious during the procedure. I don't remember it."

"Yuri," Janna grumbled.

"I'm sorry." I sheepishly smiled at Millie. "So, yeah your plan would have worked, but none of us knew they could track me without a phone."

Millie perked up.

"Sorry for being tracked or sorry for being a Russian spy or . . . whatever you are?" Janna folded her arms.

"Uh, this is all stuff I shouldn't know about." The older paramedic grabbed my shoulder firmly. "You're all patched up. Go to the hospital."

I grimaced. His strong grip hurt my entire body. I couldn't risk the hospital, though.

The paramedics headed away. The younger one made it out the door, but Agent Ben Spencer, Mr. Spencer, stopped the older one, speaking quietly to him for a minute. Afterwards, Spencer dragged the paramedic, along with a smaller agent, toward me.

The smaller agent held a device that looked like an old walkie talkie and waved it over me. "I'm going to find any tracking devices while you tell Mr. Spencer and me everything about the nuclear power plants."

The smirk never left Mr. Spencer's face as the FBI technician scanned me.

"Wait." I said, stopping the technician. "There could be a bomb in it or a poison release."

Janna's brows drew together, briefly, then she squinted. Did that mean she cared, at least a little?

"I'll only pull it if it's something I can identify," the scrawny agent said before resuming his duties. "Wouldn't your superiors have activated something like that already?"

The doctor would have, unless me turning on everyone really was something he planned for. I couldn't discern whether Sidorov displayed bravado or if he really had worked all of this out in one of his world-bending chess games.

The agent hummed to himself while he worked and listened to my story about Sidorov's plan. I turned the technician's face from incredulity to outright doubt, to understanding, and finally to fear, stopping his merry tune. I told the two men that the best thing to do was to pull every interface engine, as it mostly acted as a data interchange and wouldn't hurt anything to remove them, but they needed to make that decision on their own. I hadn't uploaded the malicious code, but that didn't mean that Sochi somehow hadn't with someone else on the inside.

The technical guy barely filled his small suit, but he handled me roughly and with surprising strength. The device buzzed in his hand more and more frequently until he settled on the back of my right shoulder. He stuck his finger on a spot and told the paramedic to cut there.

"It's okay," the agent said. "Your tracker is pretty simple and has a glass capsule. I can't see anything explosive or break-away that would indicate toxin."

"The doctor is fond of botulinum." The words rolled off my tongue without thought.

"Don't break the capsule," the agent whispered to the paramedic.

Janna tapped her foot and looked away, while Millie hugged her and looked at me with wet eyes.

I groaned but didn't move. *This is going to hurt.* I wanted the thing out, and one more cut was far preferable to losing a tooth.

"I'm not allowed to do surgery, sir." The paramedic jerked a thumb at Mr. Spencer. "He said I was helping you with something small."

"It'll *be* small. I'll cover for you if anything goes wrong." Mr. Spencer alternated his smirk between the paramedic and the spot the tech touched on my back. "It's not like anything that's happening here today actually happened." Ben tilted his head and gave a knowing look to the man.

The paramedic shook his head, then rolled his eyes.

"Good. Do you have forceps in that bag?"

The technical agent's face twisted, then turned away when the paramedic wiped my back down with alcohol in prep for the field surgery. The tech guy started scanning Janna, careful to keep his back turned away from the gruesome activity about to take place.

The paramedic poked at my back near the target location. "Ugh. It's like a cyst."

If it repulsed him, he was in the wrong business. Unfortunately, the paramedic didn't cut deep enough on his first try. I understood why they didn't let him do surgery. *Yep. He's definitely in the wrong business.* The bullet wound ached now, but I hadn't felt a thing when I had been shot. The sharp pings of pain that followed every rough cut from the paramedic tested my resolve. I fought every squirm, every desire to run away, as moving would only make it worse. Janna and Millie didn't help. Every gasp and screech from them magnified my peril in my mind.

"The wife is clear," the FBI technician said before moving onto Millie. She stiffened as he swept the scanner across her.

Relief swept over my body as the paramedic removed something from my shoulder.

"It didn't break," the paramedic said.

"Or explode," Agent Spencer said.

I relaxed enough that I could have slept, right there. Mr. Spencer grabbed the forceps from the paramedic and held it in front of my face. The small glass capsule didn't trigger any of Yuri's memories, but certainly didn't fall in his area of focus. The pain from being stitched up chased away any previous thoughts of sleep.

"This is one of *our* trackers. Isn't it?" Mr. Spencer asked, admiring the tracker.

"I think so," the smaller agent said.

"What do you think that means?" I asked sarcastically, because Janna had told him that people from every department were in on the scheme in one way or another.

"I don't think it means anything unless we can expose who's tracking it." Mr. Spencer produced a small plastic bag, dropped the capsule into it, and smirked at the device while he sealed the bag shut. "We'll see what we can find out."

"You can't trust anyone," I said to him. "There's probably someone here just looking for an opportunity to kill the three of us."

Millie yelped, making me regret my candor.

"So you keep telling me." He put his hands on his hips. "Can you give me something actionable or some names?"

"Yeah, I can give you some names."

He helped me to my feet. "Well, you'll have a lot of time to tell me while you're in custody."

I grabbed his elbow. "If you take me in, I'll be dead, and you won't learn a thing."

"You have more than a healthy amount of paranoia. We haven't even validated your story yet, Gideon." His smirk deepened. "Should I call you Gideon or Yuri?"

I looked down and whispered. "Gideon. I suppose. That's who I am now." My face flushed. I had no right to the name.

Janna and Millie stared at me blankly. They may have been out of tears to wet their eyes, so I didn't have a lot to go on how they felt. "They need more protection than you can offer."

"Paranoia and arrogance are possibly the most dangerous combination of traits a person can have. Some of this is warranted, though. If your friend Sasha hadn't matched a hundred Interpol records, I'd only be talking to your court assigned attorney right now."

"What about the nuclear power plants? You have to see that was real?" I asked.

"*I* don't understand a thing about what you said, but you scared the daylights out of Darren, here, and I made the call and shut down remote access. We have people in every reactor, manually checking for inflated levels." Mr. Spencer's perpetual smirk held its normal length. "Apparently, you can't just flip a switch and turn off a reactor, so the big heads are getting together to determine if they should begin full shutdowns as a precaution."

"So, you're a hero already," I said.

"No." His smirk lengthened. "I look like an idiot. Nothing is happening."

"*That* is a good thing. You saved more lives than you could possibly know."

Mr. Spencer's smirk did not change. "Can you hear yourself? You sound insane."

"I'm not." *I'm not?* I rolled my eyes down to the worn carpet. "Not anymore."

"The daughter is clear as well," Darren, the FBI technician, said.

"What about latent devices? There are things that lie dormant, undetectable," I said.

Darren's head reeled back. "I know." He held up his device. "With this I can see everything. I could tell if they had cancer."

Janna and Millie gasped.

Darren glanced over at them. "I was being facetious, and you don't seem to have it . . . cancer, that is," he said casually.

I *smirked* at Mr. Spencer. "Let's make a deal."

He huffed out a small laugh, then peered back at me with lowered brows. "Leave us." He gestured to Darren and the paramedic who protested that he hadn't finished with the stitches.

Mr. Spencer used his most intense stare to get the paramedic to leave.

"Project Ogon," I said, partially wiping his indestructible smirk away.

Mr. Spencer gave a sideways glance to Janna and Millie. They shrugged.

"Sochi," he said to me.

"Good. America has heard about the secret facility dedicated to their downfall."

"Go on."

I exhaled loudly. "The mastermind behind the program, Dr. Mikel Sidorov is here, in America. He was in a room at the Ahmny Hotel this morning."

"Is he still there?" Agent Spencer asked.

"No. He wouldn't be anywhere near a major city at this point. I'll give you his exit plan, but he's likely scrapped it."

"That's not much to go on," Agent Spencer said flatly.

"Mikel is Michael, from the coffee shop, by the way," I said to Janna.

She shook her head.

Millie huffed and grinned at me. "You had that one right, dad. Russian and a doctor."

"That reporter, the French guy Claude Theuriau, he convinced me something strange was going on and that he knew about the covered-up rescue operation, but I need something more concrete." Mr. Spencer rubbed his chin. "My people are going to think this is just a spy operation gone bad, and I'm starting to agree with them." He held his hand out to me, "Unless . . .."

"I know the doctor well. I can help you capture him."

Mr. Spencer shook his head slightly.

"I can help you stop him."

His eyebrows raised and his smirk uncharacteristically wavered.

"There are other teams in play. I can find them for you. I can give you everything on Project Ogon. I can give you agents, spies, and traitors to America."

"Sounds like you want something for this cooperation. That's how deals typically work. Immunity?" Mr. Spencer asked.

"No. I don't care what happens to me, other than I need to stay alive to help. Director Sidorov knows my connection to these women." *He's responsible for it. No. Not all of it.* "If he can't take me off his chess board, he'll use them to get to me."

"Spell it out for me, Gideon?"

"I want to help you and protect them, but none of us can go into your custody or your protection the normal way." I attempted my most compassionate look at Janna and Millie. "Let me help hide them away. Let me help protect them and I'll help you take down Project Ogon and everyone behind it."

"We can't live with you," Janna said in a low, strained voice. "Not after . . .."

"I know. I'm not suggesting that."

"We have a say in what happens to us. We didn't do anything wrong." Janna's face flushed; her hands tightened into fists.

I closed my eyes. I *needed* them to be safe. "Of course you have a say. I—"

"This is all well and good," Mr. Spencer broke in with a raised voice, then lowered it to a harsh hush. "But I'm just a field agent. My brain can't fathom how I'd manage any of this. I don't even know what rules or laws I'd be bending, or breaking, for a start."

"You'll help me help them?" I asked.

Janna's mouth gaped and she shook her head at me. "I'm not going anywhere you say to. You need to be in jail for everything you've done."

"I know." I glanced at Agent Spencer. "For this and more, but putting any of us in the system will get us killed."

Millie looked at me with an almost smile, again giving me hope.

Mr. Spencer regarded them both, one hand casually on his hip. "I'm open to something. If half of what he says is true, it's worth taking some extra precautions. We can't deny the danger people like Sasha pose."

My shoulders relaxed.

"Jansen," Mr. Spencer called over his shoulder, out the front door, then jerked back to me. "Is Maria Jansen on your list?" he asked with a low voice.

I searched through names in Yuri's memory. "I don't think so."

"You don't think so?" Mr. Spencer tossed his hands up. "Never mind. Whatever. She's a good colleague of mine. I trust her, but you need to give me something."

Something more than foiling a plot to destroy America?

Maria shut the door behind her then engaged Agent Spencer in a private discussion.

Janna and Millie took the opportunity to argue over the merits of custody and the witness protection program. At least they acknowledged that everything they knew about the process came from movies, books, and television.

I searched Yuri's memory for something big to bargain with, a sleeper agent, a safe house, an urgent plot, more assets like me, bank accounts; Yuri would have died before divulging any of this information, even under duress or drugs, but I could pull it all as if it were a simple Internet search. *Did you plan for this, Sidorov?* Any one of these things would make a field agent's career, but what would help the most? *A mole. A big one that would shake Sochi and America.* Would he believe me?

Mr. Spencer handed a phone to me. Maria looked at the ground, her face red.

"This is Agent Jansen's side phone." He shrugged. "Department phones have their challenges. My private cell is in there, and yes, I can track this thing. The two of us are going to stash you for a while. Do not burn me on this."

"I won't."

"So what? You're really doing this? You're letting him go?" Janna asked.

Mr. Spencer didn't look her in the eye. "I can take you into custody right now, against your will, but I don't want to make that choice for you. I was assigned this case because it was high profile with the press and our office felt something didn't add up with Gideon's capture and rescue. We knew Russia had a hand played here, but nothing like Gideon is saying. There's enough here to believe . . . to believe him."

"Director Raymond," I said.

"Andrew B. Raymond, Director of the Federal Bureau of Investigation," Mr. Spencer said flatly, his smirk nearing his ear with this news. "That's a big claim. Dammit Gideon, give me something real." He jerked a hand toward Janna and Millie. "And, in front of them? Come on."

Maria mirrored his smirk. They must have worked together a lot.

"There was a meeting, ten years ago, in Sochi. There's documentation, money, and blackmail. I can get you all of it. Well, I'll need a little help."

"Jesus, Gideon, maybe you're right, and we'll do what we can, but that's way above our pay grades. We'll . . . talk . . . about this." He gestured to Maria.

"Sochi. Ogon," popped out of my mouth as soon as the thought formed. *The waterways project shows promise. The electrical grid would reap the most reward.* "We can stop another scheme similar to mine."

"Go on," Agent Jansen said.

Mr. Spencer peered at me, nodding.

I glanced at Janna. With her head down and fists tight, she mumbled to herself, probably trying to get a handle on everything, or plotting my demise. I wouldn't blame her for the latter.

It burned me that I wasn't finished causing her pain.

Millie returned the glance I gave her. She seemed full of energy and on the tips of her toes, looking at me expectantly, hanging on my words.

I turned to Maria. "This other mission of theirs is centered around the U.S. electrical grid. These operatives have been embedded longer than I was and likely don't know they're operatives at this point."

"You'll take us through every step, once we get you away," Maria said.

"Of course." I looked at Janna, then Millie. "What about them"

Agent Spencer looked at Janna, gaining her attention. "I know a place, if you're okay with it."

Janna's face twisted into a pained frown, her eyes on the verge of tears, the rest of her body rigid as a board. She said nothing, only giving the slightest of nods in acceptance.

Penance. An Epilogue.

I looked across the room at my mom. Here, like every day at Ben's friend's fishing cabin, she just sat in a chair, staring out the window. Initially, with her anger, she had us making three meals a day and cleaning this place, but lately she had drifted away. Her attitude reminded me of the first days after Dad had been taken. I hadn't been much better back then, but it was she who pulled me out of it. I leaned on her strength until I found my own.

"Mom," I called. No response.

The cabin's interior was nice, but gross at the same time. Mounted fish on the walls turned my stomach if I stared at them too long. The rest of the main room could have been fine, maybe fun, with the fake log cabin walls, large fireplace, and huge open ceiling. But, whoever owned the place had an obsession with dark wood and leather. The couch that I sprawled on, dark wood and leather. The chairs in front of the fireplace, dark wood and leather. The table Mom sat at, only dark wood. Her chair had leather, though.

Boredom gnawed at me. I stood up and perused the short bookshelf for the millionth time. Still, nothing but stupid fishing and hunting magazines lay on the dusty shelves. Some worn paperback books leaned against a bookend, but nothing grabbed my attention except maybe a series about a wizard detective. *I'm not that bored yet.* I went back to the only book I'd brought with me, on the couch, *The Return of the King*, but I didn't want to read.

"Mom," I called to her again with no response.

I walked next to her and rested my hand on her shoulder. In a softer voice, I tried again.

"Yes, Millie," she finally said.

"How do we deal with things, Mom?" I asked.

"I don't know." She wouldn't look at me. Mom only stared into nothingness these past weeks. Or had it been a month? Or months?

"No. Mom. How do we deal with things?" I asked, not hiding my irritation.

She finally looked at me. "What?"

"How do we deal with things?"

"I don't . . .."

"You taught me how to handle this pain." I folded my arms and looked away. "Don't give up on us. I need you."

My mom sniffled, then croaked out some words. "I'm sorry, Millie. Nothing makes sense anymore. What do you need?"

"I just need you. I'm going crazy here."

She stood and hugged me, leaning her head on my shoulder. I hadn't noticed how tall I'd grown until that moment, maybe as tall as Mom.

"Do you want to go for a walk?" she asked.

"Yeah." I looked out the window. The midday sun barely made an impact through the overcast sky. The weather seemed to match Mom's mood. It didn't matter if we got a little rain on us. I needed something to do.

We grabbed our coats; Mom donned her gloves. I opened the door and stepped out. Immediately, the burble of the river and spiciness of pine welcomed me to the great outdoors. My mind drifted to geocaching, but Ben had said that we couldn't do those types of activities, maybe for a long time. Taking a deep breath, I relished the cool, fresh air over the staleness in the cabin.

We followed a mulched, half-mile path down to the river. Other trails existed, but the FBI wouldn't let us take them. I laughed to myself. Not the FBI, just two somewhat rogue agents, who didn't instill confidence.

"What's so funny?" my mom asked.

She noticed?

"Our life."

"True that," she said, but didn't join in the laughter.

Pine needles masked the now familiar path in front of us, fallen from the hundreds of trees that filled the picturesque landscape. I never focused on this stuff before, but all this time in my head had made me somewhat of an intellectual, although none of the adults in my life would agree. To Mom, Ben, and Maria, I was still just a child, even though I'd lived through more than most with my dad's kidnapping and . . .. Oh, and how could they dismiss being almost killed by that psycho, Sasha? Experiencing these events, surviving them, over the past year had forced me to grow up, whether they saw it or not.

We made our way down to the river. Only the light rustle of our footsteps competed with the river and the occasional chirp of a bird. Mom's silence didn't help me keep my focus and I thought of him again. Mom had forbidden me from talking about him, but I kept challenging her. I *needed* to talk about him, to try and figure out who he was and why he seemingly threw away his entire life for us. My gut told me that he was a good person, but Mom couldn't see past his betrayal and could only describe him as evil.

He killed my father. Tears welled in my eyes, but I couldn't tell if the pain and sorrow were from my father dying or for the death of our relationship that happened long before that. Both hurt. I couldn't face the last thing I said to my dad without crying. I had told him that I hated him for canceling on me for the millionth time. A tear rolled down my cheek. The sky opened up in a light mist, crying along with me.

"What's wrong, baby?" Mom asked.

"You don't want to know."

"By moving forward," she said.

"What?" I asked.

"Earlier. You asked how we deal with things," she said.

"By moving forward." I wiped away the extra tears from my cheeks and willed all but a single one away. "I'm sad for *him*. I miss him."

"Don't," she said, almost growling.

I knew it hurt her, but something inside of me told me the man who had come into our lives was a good person. This man could never hurt someone like Sasha would. It had to be like *he* said, that the man who had caused us so much suffering, Yuri, was gone. His time with us couldn't be a lie. And, despite what the agents believed, we couldn't hide from master Russian spies forever. We needed *his* help if we were going to find a way through this. We still had the burner phone, but I couldn't figure out a way to contact him, yet, or I would have. *He. Him. What do I even call him? Yuri? Gideon? Dad? Yurideon?*

"We can't just pretend like he doesn't exist," I said.

"Millie. You're too young to understand." Mom's cheeks flushed. *There it is. I'm a child.*

"We can't forgive him for what . . .." Mom drifted off, looking through the woods.

"Forgiveness isn't for him. It's for u—"

Mom shushed me.

"Okay. Rude," I said more to myself, looking away from her. How could she dismiss me so easily? Should I bide my time and be patient? Anger welled up in me. *No.* My mom needed to acknowledge my feelings about this.

"You need—"

She grabbed my arm and pulled me toward her, hurting me. Too shocked to say anything, I gaped in astonishment.

"That car," she whispered, pointing through the trees.

Immediately, cold sweat hit the back of my neck. Through the trees, sure enough, a dark sedan sat still. Alarms went off in my head, because we were at least a mile away from any roads. Neither Maria nor Ben were scheduled to come today. They'd relegated their visits to once a week as they worked through whom they could trust and how to protect us long term. *Turns out, they can't even protect us short term. Dad . . . Yuri was right.*

We stared at the car for several moments, waiting for someone to exit the vehicle or for any movement in the forest. After several moments of nothing, Mom tapped me and pointed toward the river.

"Let's head upstream toward the bait shop. It's only a couple of miles. I'll text Ben," Mom whispered. She typed the message out on her phone, then we headed toward the river.

"You don't want to go back to the cabin?" I asked as quietly as I could.

"No. That car is facing the cabin. Whoever it is could be there already."

"Ben's friend?" I asked.

"Let's hope so," Mom said.

We walked as discreetly as we could several feet before Mom received a reply from Ben. She froze after reading it.

"We need to run, Millie."

What?

She grabbed the back of my jacket and pushed me forward until I ran on my own.

My feet seemed to move without me telling them to. I grunted as I did my best to not fall down and keep up with my mom, who kept looking over her shoulder.

"Faster," she yelled.

Behind us, a car started, its engine revved, and tires spun in the dirt.

I glanced over my shoulder at the vehicle. It couldn't drive through the trees, but we also didn't have a better option than running aimlessly through the forest. Whoever drove the car could follow us all the way to the bait shop.

"Mom," I shrieked.

"Keep running," she screamed back, "no matter what."

I'd found my footing and no longer had trouble keeping up with Mom. The mist added to the already muddy riverbank, but there were enough river rocks to keep from slipping or sticking. My focus remained on running and not on the person chasing us. Oddly, the crackle of the car tires driving over terrain stopped.

Two gunshots echoed through the river valley.

I turned to look over my shoulder and lost my balance, skidding on the riverbank. My palms and knees screamed with pain.

Mom ripped me back up to my feet. She tugged on my arms, screaming at me to keep running, but her voice seemed distant. I panted heavily, barely able to breathe. I wanted to tell her I was sorry, but I couldn't speak.

After tugging on me a few more times, Mom broke down into tears and hugged me. "It's okay, honey. It's okay." She repeated the lines over and over while I remained frozen except for my shaky breaths.

"You have your Yuri to thank for this," a man yelled emerging from the woods, his gun pointed at the ground. His accent sounded much like Michael's from the coffee shop.

Mom placed herself between the man and me. I remained stiff as a board.

I didn't know him. He walked with a limp, wore black suit pants and a white long sleeved dress shirt, half untucked and half covered in blood. The man raised his gun in our direction.

"Well then. Are you going to kill us?" Mom asked.

No. It can't be over.

"Not yet." The words rolled off the man's tongue in his thick accent.

"Who are you?" Mom asked.

"Who I am is difficult question to answer these days," the man said with cold, dead eyes. "I was man on a mission. Now, I am man who needs revenge."

The sound of another car came from beyond the trees. Its tires dug up the ground and its brakes squealed.

"That would be the FBI," Mom said.

"Not FBI," the man said. He smirked. "Yuri."

The man motioned with his gun, trying to get us to move, but I couldn't budge. He limped closer, then grabbed for my jacket, but Mom attacked his arm. He shoved her to the ground, then pointed his gun at me.

"Enough," he said calmly, like his horrible actions were a normal everyday affair. "Stand up," he ordered Mom. She complied, again placing herself between me and him.

This time, when he motioned us to move with his gun, Mom was able to move me toward the tree line where two black cars now waited, and a man walked through the trees toward us. Our assailant breathed heavily behind us.

"Leave them alone," a familiar voice yelled from the trees.

"The doctor was right about you. That you would come running because you fell in love with these women."

Yuri, Dad, whoever he was, emerged from the trees. He wore jeans and a heavy jacket, but did not limp or appear wounded, like our assailant. He pointed a handgun toward the man, and unfortunately, us.

"Andrey, let them go," Dad said.

"Maybe. Maybe not until after I kill you." Andrey exhaled, loudly. "Yuri."

"You don't care about them. You only want me, Andrey."

The cold air, the mist, my numb brain, all of it kept my feet frozen to the ground as my body shivered. Between heartbeats, I feared I'd died. It seemed like I would die before Andrey got around to killing me.

Andrey groaned behind me. I didn't dare glance at him, even if I could move.

"You may have already killed me, Yuri." He moaned some more. "This wound does not . . . does not look good."

"Nobody else has to get hurt. Let's finish it. Just us."

Andrey laughed. "Everyone thought that you were best of program in Sochi, the smartest, the strongest, but I knew the truth."

"Oh, and what's that?" Gideon asked.

"You were the weakest," Andrey said.

Gideon moved forward prompting Andrey to push his gun into the back of my neck. Feet shuffled behind me while Mom cried, "No." I shivered even more, causing my teeth to rattle.

"Ah. Ah," Andrey warned, followed by Gideon stopping and pointing his gun away.

"You were so needy of Sidorov's love that you pushed yourself harder than any of us." Andrey pushed the gun harder against my neck. "Always first. Always helping. We all hated you, save Sasha."

My stomach turned. All I could do was shiver and be sick. "Dad," I cried out.

"Dad." Andrey laughed again. "Oh these poor women. And I thought you had wronged me."

"I didn't wrong you, Andrey. I just stopped Sidorov's—"

"And robbed me of my glory." The man spat.

My body added swaying to its list of approved movements. With all the hyperventilating, I grew lightheaded.

"I do not hate these women, and Sidorov told me he did not care if they lived or died."

Michael. Everyone has hurt us so much.

"Then let us go. He's here," Mom said.

Andrey coughed, briefly turning it into a laugh, but the cough won out. "Would it be cliche if I wanted to hurt you to hurt him?" He managed to chuckle without coughing. "The doctor said Yuri would come out if I threatened you. That was enough for me."

"I did come when the FBI intercepted your messages. Ask yourself how we were able to do that. Sidorov doesn't make mistakes and I almost stopped you." Dad gripped his handgun with both hands but didn't raise it toward us. "He wants you dead. And if all you want is me dead, then why did you run when I was right there?"

"For advantage," Andrey said. He opened fire, bullets seemingly whizzing over my shoulder.

Mom pulled me down into a crouch.

Andrey yanked me up and dragged me backward with him. Mom came at him fast. He kicked her back and shoved the gun at the side of my head. "Stop," he said.

Mom groaned but stopped her attack; tears ran down her face. Andrey pointed his gun to the tree line, Dad nowhere to be seen.

"Come out, Yuri," Andrey said, his breath on the side of my face, repulsing me and freezing me with fear once again. "If you hide, I'll hurt them." He moaned and wavered. "And I'm running short on time, old friend."

He's going to die, and he's going to take us all with him.

"Sidorov wants us all to die, you included," Dad said.

Andrey fired a shot in the direction of the voice. I ducked down, screaming, but Andrey jerked me up straight. My ears rang.

He's never going to let us go. Surrender to the inevitable. Surrender.

"You're just like a pawn in one of his chess games. He sacrificed me, Sasha, Dmitri, and now you."

The sound of Andrey's teeth grinding filled my ears. "You killed Dmitri. Not the doctor. And, worst of all, you betrayed and killed your Sasha."

"You're wrong," Mom's voice tapered into a high pitch, as if she questioned her own words. "I killed Sasha."

"What?" Andrey pulled his gun away from me, and I found the courage to look over my shoulder. He had the gun positioned halfway between Mom and me.

Surrender to your . . . success. I lunged for Andrey's handgun, but he moved faster, wrenching me back with his other hand and pointing the gun back toward me.

"No," Mom screamed, lunging for Andrey, and knocking his gun hand down.

The rest of my fear left me, along with all emotion. *Surrender.* I simply moved.

Fighting free from Andrey's grip, I grappled his forearm, wrapping my upper body around it. Clawing and digging my nails into his hand failed to make him release his weapon. He struck my back. *No pain. No fear.* Mom attacked more furiously, keeping him from hitting me more. He cursed and screamed but wouldn't let the handgun go. I buried my teeth in his hand, just behind the thumb. The gun discharged, deafening me, but I only bit harder.

Andrey struck Mom hard. As she fell, she grabbed his jacket sleeve and tugged it to the ground with her. He crashed into me, and we both tumbled to the ground. His agonizing cry echoed through the river valley. As impossible as it seemed, I bit down even harder—he dropped the gun.

He slipped free from his jacket and staggered back as I scrambled for his gun. Soaked with Andrey's blood, I couldn't get a grip on it. Mom grabbed the handgun from my fumbling hands. Everything moved as if in slow motion, between heartbeats. I looked back to Andrey, half his shirt covered in blood. He reached behind his back and produced another handgun. He raised his gun toward us. Mom screamed and raised hers.

Before either of them fired a shot, Andrey dropped to his knees. Three new spots of blood grew on his already soaked white shirt. Andrey's eyes grew distant, and he fell forward, landing face down, unmoving.

My ears still only rang, but the muffled sounds of Mom yelling at Dad had begun to come through.

I hadn't noticed that I was on my knees, looking up at the two of them. The pain from the river rocks smashed against my legs won out, and I stood.

"How many times will we be used? When is it over, Yuri?" my mom yelled, placing herself between me and him.

"I'm not him anymore, Janna." He squatted down and rolled Andrey over, checking him and pocketing some of the items found, like a phone and another tiny device. He stood. "I'm fixing things, Janna. This one got through, but at least we confirmed that they can find you."

"Well thank God for that," Mom said sarcastically, throwing her hands in the air.

"Thank you for coming," I said, earning a horrified look from Mom.

"I promise that I'll fix everything, Millie," he said.

I believed him.

"Nobody—" Mom inhaled deeply, like she wanted to breathe fire "—nobody can fix any of this.

"And you." Mom turned on Dad. "How are you able to just run free? You should be in prison."

"I'm not free, but not exactly in custody. I left . . . against their wishes . . . and kind of stole one of their cars—" he held up the gun "—and Maria's gun, when we found out Andrey was coming. I needed to act faster than they could, and I almost stopped him." Dad curled his nose at Andrey. "I'm going to be in trouble, but they didn't understand the threat like I did."

He held out car keys to Mom. "Take these. Take my car and meet Ben where you said you would. Nobody else is coming."

"Are you spying on Ben, now?" Mom asked.

"I have to." Dad looked down, shaking his head. "It's impossible to trust anyone."

"Tell me about it," she said.

Mom grabbed my hand and hauled me away from the riverbank and through the woods. I spared a glance over my shoulder at Dad, knowing he wasn't my actual father. His face was pale, and his forehead creased. The mist made it difficult to tell, but his eyes seemed on the edge of tears as he watched us leave.

I know Mom didn't, couldn't trust this man, but I did. He would never hurt us. All he wanted to do was make us safe. As weird and wrong as these feelings were, I believed that he did love us. Mom released her vice grip on my hand as the terrain demanded her attention.

My world would feel a lot safer if I had a way to communicate with him. *I'll find a way.* I spun around to look at him one last time. His slumped posture betrayed the pain he must be feeling. I gripped one hand in the other and held them outward toward him, then over my heart.

His eyes widened and he grinned, mirroring my gesture.

I turned away and followed my mom through the trees.

Even with all the pain that I'd been through, that Mom had been through, I believed his life to be more tragic. We'd need his help if we were going to survive. *I mean, is it selfish that I don't care if the country survives as long as Mom and I do?* But I supposed Agent Spencer, the F.B.I., and the rest of America needed him too.

This man, Yuri, Dad, Gideon, though, he needed us.

Konets

Read on to the next page for a preview of John Hardt's next book, a science fiction story with literal star-crossed lovers.

Nirmana

Ancient History

Khali followed her mother down the dimly lit corridor to the Knowledge Hall entrance. As they reached the end, the large, familiar metal etching loomed before her. Ardently admiring the engravings and knowing that her mother detested the historical scenes for what they represented, not to mention her mother's depiction within, Khali couldn't hide her wonderment, brightening her face. She read the titles aloud. "*The Surrender of the Derg* and *The Peace of Andelor."*

Her mother sighed but refrained from her usual lecture that the very existence of etchings like these meant to bring the Derg low and place their people, the Shandi, high. Such garish displays contrasted with the ideals of the Shandi. Celebrating heroes, victory, and dominance were attributes Mother felt the Shandi could do without. Victory followed as a result of the Shandi performing their duty. Heroes did not exist, because every Shandi always behaved admirably, and forcing an advisory's submission, as the Shandi had done with the Derg, devolved into a situation where a stronger people exercised dominance over a weaker society.

Drifting her eyes and hand across the raised surface in further admiration, Khali settled on the depiction of her mother, Commander Maya, who stood, etched proudly, in the second row of military leaders. Khali whispered, "The Hero of Motilee."

"You know I despise that adulation."

Her mother's stern look and strong words squelched Khali's hope that the fire burning within Khali also burned in her mother. It had to be there. They shared so many traits. Why couldn't her mother accept that she was special and worthy of the hope and admiration she gave their people?

"I only did my duty, as you would have, as any of us would."

"Many say that without your actions, millions would have perished. We would have lost the colonies across the Kee'ler Flats and would have faced a prolonged, costly war." Khali raised her chin in anticipation of her mother's response.

Her mother huffed, then said, "Millions did perish. Just not our people." Her mother's words trailed off and she stared distantly, seemingly past the etching. "The Shandi paid a different price . . .."

The Shandi certainly had paid in blood and other costs, but none more so than Khali and her mother. Khali bit her bottom lip, driving away the memory of what simply performing her duty had cost her mother, and Khali, that day. A Shandi should be proud to pay such costs, but Khali never felt pride, only pain.

Furthermore, a distance had formed between them as a result of the conflict, driving her mother deeper and deeper into her duty as Commander, but not as mother. It had been a long time since they had spent any real time together. The last good memory happened before Khali had been assigned to command school. Now that she had finished her education, Khali had the opportunity to repair their broken relationship.

Arguing with her mother about her role in the battle wouldn't help mend, nor would attempting to speak to the commander about her or her daughter's feelings. With the emotional void between them, Khali yearned to truly understand her mother, to heat the thoughts that caused her to stare blankly in recollection.

Alas, with all of Khali's skills, she had not mastered the ability to break through her mother's formidable barriers. Khali cleared her throat to bring her mother back to the moment.

Blinking, her mother wrinkled her brow and scanned Khali's face. She shook her head and spoke, "Details of the war with the Derg is a lesson for another day. You are apprenticed to command, and I am your mentor. You have the immense honor and responsibility to lead and thereby grow the greatness of the Shandi."

Her mother never talked about the famous battles or the war. Outside of what they had personally lost, Khali had to learn about the conflict on her own. Did her mother truly think her part so insignificant? That every Shandi would have behaved the same? That her actions were not special? Khali huffed.

"Is there something you wish to say?" her mother asked.

With wide eyes, Khali looked up to her mother. "No, Commander."

Her mother looked back at the etching. "Good. I promise that I will discuss this conflict with you, but not today."

Khali squinted at her mother. Was there a deeper reason why her mother did not speak of the battle at Motilee? Many Shandi suffered losses that day. Khali had lost just as much as anyone, and tragically, she lost any semblance of a mother that day.

Even though Khali had experienced firsthand what the life of a soldier could cost, could change in a person, she couldn't help but idolize her mother. She followed in her mother's footsteps and dedicated every moment of her life to be assigned the role of leader, to command. It was not the Shandi way, but Khali craved the same recognition her mother had received more than anything.

Would recognition and equal footing break down the wall her mother had placed between them? How could she hope to match the *Hero of Motilee*? It would take a distinguished military career, one with glory through conflict, of which Khali sought. Regretfully, their current assignment would not present any opportunities for distinction.

The silence of the entryway brought Khali's attention back to her mother who held her palm open toward the etchings. She dismissed the etchings with a wave and a snarl. A small tight frown preceded the gloss of her eyes. Her mother looked at Khali. "There is nothing to learn from embellished pieces of art. Today we discuss the role of the Shandi in the cosmos."

"We are a mining ship. We don't have a role in the cosmos." Khali didn't try to hide her disappointment. "With your status, you could have received any assignment. Why this? There's nothing out there."

"Without resources, what are the Shandi?" Her mother raised a brow, but her otherwise blank expression conveyed that she expected no reply. "There is more than you can see for our people out *there*." Her mother folded her arms in front of her and tapped her forearm. "What more could you seek?"

"Nothing, Commander."

"Good. We have the lesson. Sociology."

Her mother led Khali past four identical, large rooms within the Knowledge Hall before entering an even larger nondescript area. Each of the rooms they passed could be dynamically configured for whatever purpose a Shandi required, often for training, education, or proctoring.

The room came to light and life, containing a single exhibit. Coincidentally, or not, each item displayed represented the compilation of everything the Shandi had recorded about the race known as "The Derg." Digital displays and holographic representations hovered throughout the large, interactive room with more etchings adorning the walls.

A quick survey of the data revealed information about the Derg's known population densities, their current territories and systems, their technical and military capabilities, their resource needs and where they acquired them, their food sources, and diet. Scattered throughout, pedestals broadcast holographic representations of Derg technology, weapons, and models of their ships.

The central holographic display, which contained life-size holograms of a male and female Derg, drew Khali toward it.

Her mother held prominence and respect among the Shandi because of the Derg but never passed any knowledge about them onto her daughter. Seeing them, so life-like, brought to mind their violent tendencies and history. She did not fear them, but they did cause Khali discomfort.

The Derg had long, lean limbs with thick skin, almost leather-like, not thin like her own. Their beaked noses were nearly avian in their structure. Overall, their faces resembled a predator—complete with two rows of sharp teeth.

Fate and evolution controlled their visage, but if their survival as a species relied on intimidation, then their once frightening presence dwindled in Khali eyes. Their existence as a whole seemed limited and, in a pitying way, weak, leaving them innocuous to her. A species could not control how it evolved, not on an individual basis. Still, she wouldn't want to meet one in a darkened corridor.

She extended her palm to the display and then toward the male Derg. The image brightened to signal she had selected it. Changing her gesture to extend two fingers in the direction of the digital representation, Khali flicked left to scroll through different samples.

Seeing the variances, she could not help but frown. It made her uncomfortable how they altered their appearance. Derg commonly self-mutilated, inked their skin, grew their hair to extremes and integrated technology into their biology, at times for ceremony, to memorialize accomplishment, and sometimes simply to intimidate others.

The Derg commonly used biological manipulation to augment their capabilities, overcoming genetic limitations. Some had replaced their eyes with enhanced implants. Others replaced limbs in the same manner. A handful even went as far as meddling with neural implants.

These grotesque, unnecessary behaviors changed the definition of the Derg, abandoning their true natures in an ill-fated search for distinction. In losing themselves, they had lost what it meant to be a Derg, so much so that nobody could determine what that truly meant anymore. Their entire society had lost their way. Without a unified purpose, without an identity, they would never discover their people's truest embodiment as the Shandi had.

Her mother launched into the lecture. "As a leader, you need to think about our neighboring species with a different focus. The Derg establish prominence through wealth and combat. This base motivation made them foolish enough to go to war with us. As a result, we have limited their capabilities and are monitoring them continually. The Derg are no longer a true threat, if they ever were, but that does not mean you shouldn't be prepared to deal with them in the future." Mother proceeded to the next room, presumably to not spend any more time than necessary with her former enemy.

Khali lingered and stared at an etching, barely acknowledging the details of the battle scene depicted upon it. The violent image showed Derg fighting Derg, but the overall message, outside of hostility, diminished. The metal work of art matched the style of the one in the entry hall. Had they provided the famous etchings as part of some bizarre ritual to commemorate their defeat? Or did they revel in the event more than the outcome? She would have to investigate the origin of the entryway etching at a later time.

She was well aware of the Derg and their perpetual provocations, and how they had been constantly threatening and harassing her people. Testing the Shandi defenses had become a recurring event. They mistook Shandi inaction for weakness—to their own detriment. It all seemed foolish and wasteful, unless their motivations centered around the conflict itself and not in victory. Then, in a way, Khali could make some sense of it.

Their peculiar culture raised their young to battle one another, often to the death. Throughout their lives, they perpetually fought amongst themselves, keeping their society in a constant state of conflict, bringing riches to few while the vast majority suffered and did without. A society such as theirs could never satisfy its thirst for war.

As much as Khali craved a similar glory through conflict, being remotely Derg-like turned something in her stomach. Thoughts of ever meeting a Derg and being forced to indulge their sick fascination with battle lessened the glory somehow and flipped her motivation upside-down. How could she claim victory if they had already won just by participating in a fight? How could she be a hero if she celebrated in the death in the same manner as them?

With her mother's relatively recent conflict, the suffering the Derg caused her people, what Khali lost as a result, and this horrible realization of their core motivation, Khali shuddered—she hated them.

No. Her bias against them clouded her clarity. A good commander must have clarity. And she didn't hate them; she hated the voice within her that thirsted for battle, like them. She needed to be better than that.

Khali hurried after her mother into the next room, seeing her for the first time with new understanding of why she did not play the hero. The purpose of the instruction in the Knowledge Hall was wholly intended to be a scripted education, shaping another new commander for the Shandi Sovereignty, but Khali had gained something deeper, something unexpected, something that brought her closer to her mother, in addition to getting to spend time with her.

Khali's assignment to her mother came about because of the natural connection they shared and Khali's abilities. The Shandi people hoped to create another Commander Maya and the Sovereignty agreed, but Khali struggled and fought to reach this moment if only to hear her mother's voice again. After so much time apart, seeing her mother, let alone speak with her, had become a luxury.

The next exhibit lit up in similar fashion with a different species less familiar to Khali even though she had heard of them. The Kyru or "tut-tuts" as Shandi children called them because of their resemblance to the amphibious creatures inhabiting many of the Shandi controlled regions.

Adult Kyru were much shorter than her people, with overly muscular arms and legs but portly everywhere else—especially in the midsection. At first glance, their large eyes appeared completely black, but closer inspection revealed a darker pupil and iris. Sparse, thin hair, barely perceptible, coated their pale green skin.

Khali scrolled through the representations. Other than the size difference between genders, Khali couldn't discern much difference among individuals. Instead of etchings on the walls, schematics, diagrams, and formulas hung.

Changing her attention to the Kyru's technology holograms, Khali admired the large sensor arrays and botanical structures. Their conservatories matched Shandi structures of the same purpose. Nothing resembled a weapon on any of their impressive stations or transport ships.

"The Kyru. For all known history, they have been dedicated to scientific pursuits. They have given us much, as we have them. Together we have unlocked many secrets of the universe. We provide them protection and resources for they are the oldest, truest friends of the Shandi. A commander should seek their wisdom when bereft of answers." Without adding any more information, her mother turned and left.

Khali smirked at the display as her fascination with the nuances of their technology wore off. Boredom won out, and Khali followed her mother into the next room.

The next exhibit came to life as she entered, displaying a species entirely foreign to Khali. Similar in height and body frame to the Shandi, with faint blue skin consistent with her people, their large heads stood out in contrast. Their mouths seemed to extend along their entire jawline, mere slits for eyes, and exceptionally large nostrils flattened against their exaggerated faces.

The Derg looked menacing. The Kyru looked friendly. This species evoked no immediate feelings. Flipping through examples of *The Taraks* revealed quite a bit of variation in height, weight and facial construction.

Nothing hung on the walls as representative artwork. No holograms displayed unique technology specific to their race. Interestingly, though, the Taraks exceeded the Derg's need for individuality, as not two of the Taraks' ships were alike. Obvious weapons adorned every vessel, helping Khali easily determine their intent.

"The Taraks we have encountered have been pirates or scavengers. Our understanding is that they have no government to speak of. They seem to be nomadic as they have no permanent home, taking over abandoned colonies for a time, then moving on. Not a major threat, but they have caused problems for colonies and ships that were in trouble from time to time. Their weapons are large, but do not challenge the weakest ship in the Sovereignty. Remain diligent and they should avoid us. If a conflict seems imminent, exhaust diplomacy before attacking. Usually, they just need our help. Give it to them."

Her mother turned from the exhibit and folded her arms behind her. The thick bands that encircled each of Mother's arms stood out in contrast to her otherwise plain white uniform. The bands represented the distinction Commander Maya had earned within the Shandi. On her left arm, four navy bands signified command of a ship, but they paled in significance against the jagged, red and navy band on her right arm that recognized her acceptance into the Honor Guard.

Khali glanced at her own left arm, with three thin stripes, denoting a junior commander. No other ornamentation adorned Khali's uniform. The thirst for battle may have shrunk inside of her, but not her thirst for distinction. She shouldn't want to stand out, but she did just the same. The words of her people echoed in her mind. *There is no self. There is only the Shandi.* The belief had carried her people through thousands of years of prosperity. Who was she to challenge this truth? Why did she need to be so special?

Abruptly, her mother turned and stood close to Khali.

A little shorter, Khali took half a step back to lessen the contrast.

"I expect you to fully understand each known alien race," her mother said. "More than my commentary and opinions, I need you to understand their characteristics, their data sets, their motivations and their history with the Shandi. A dutiful commander understands her allies and potential adversaries. Study them with a leader's eye from all angles, threats, positions and learn the lessons from the past."

"Yes, Commander. I will be thorough."

Her mother's posture loosened. "I know you will." A shadow of a smile briefly appeared on her lips.

Khali's heart raced as she reveled in the small sliver of acceptance.

Her mother led them to the next room.

The room assembled itself on their arrival revealing a species Khali had familiarity with, but not in vivid detail. The room seemed to darken with the realization of who they were: the villains in the tales Shandi parents told their children to scare them into fulfilling their duties.

Her mother said their name with disgust, "The Mak'Tar."

The stories preceded any living Shandi by a thousand generations, but everyone agreed they really existed. The Mak'Tar were easily the worst beings that had ever inhabited the galaxy. The impact of their brutality still reverberated within the Shandi Sovereignty. As a child, Khali had twisted their image into the stuff of nightmare; though seeing them represented like this, they seemed smaller, less capable, almost weak.

Identical to the Shandi in most respects, where Khali had pale blue skin, theirs seemed soft and grey, with a mildly reflective faded sheen. Her people had shiny, black hair in contrast to the silver hair decorating the representations before them. Something about their ears felt off, possibly they were smaller on average, or their cartilage followed a different structure. She could not place enough of a difference. Reflexively, Khali traced the outside of her ear to study the contrast.

Artwork, paintings and sculptures, hung on or hovered near the walls. The styles and subjects varied with a beauty, haunting beauty considering the artists, equal to anything the Shandi had created. A single wooden carving, larger than the Derg metal etching, hung in the center of one wall. The carving depicted a woman, holding a wreath above her head.

Khali's eyes widened when she moved on to the depictions of the Mak'Tar vessels. They matched the nightmarish reputation of the Mak'Tar, resembling animals more than machinery; some even seemed to have teeth. A kind of exoskeleton covered the largest vessel and its entire hull slanted and narrowed toward the nose. The front culminated into four sharp points like an aggressive maw. Khali reached toward the hologram but pulled back for fear that if she put her hand too close to the mandibles, it would bite her.

Khali moved closer to the models of their people and cycled through the variations. She tilted her head and studied a Mak'Tar woman. Examining her own hands, she ran one down the back of the other. She then regarded her own being and that of her mother. Her mother's physique almost identically matched the muscular stature of the typical Mak'Tar female. The similarities between the Mak'Tar and the Shandi contrasted with her childhood prejudice. These people were certainly not the same villains of childhood fantasy that persisted in her head.

Each of them had Shandi-like noses, mouths, and eyes. Their omnivorous teeth with a single sharp incisor on each side could do no more damage than Khali's own. The shapes of their heads matched the typical Shandi. The color of their hair did not match, but the texture seemed to. Each had two arms, two legs, ten fingers and ten toes in similar proportions. If Khali dyed her hair, and powdered her skin, she could pass for a Mak'Tar. Khali was about to mention this to her mother, but it seemed as if she were to speak.

Her mother continued with her tone of disdain. "Though we have not encountered them for nearly two hundred thousand cycles, every Shandi knows of them. This is the race that nearly eliminated our people from existence. As you know, they decimated our original home, Jya, making it unlivable to this day.

"*They* poisoned our food, using famine and disease as a weapon. *They* used our own people against us. They infiltrated us, tearing our society apart. They assassinated our leaders. They lied, broke truces and used weapons of unimaginable power." Mother tapered off her cadence and demanded eye contact. "*They* enslaved millions of our people.

"You know most of this. Through this peril, our true society was born. Irivat and The First escaped from slavery and turned the tide. They pursued the Mak'Tar relentlessly and eliminated their threat once and for all. After so much time, we never expect to see their kind again."

Khali squinted at the female representation of the Mak'Tar. "Why do you think they did this to us?"

"We are told that they were chiefly motivated by greed, like the Derg. They took it further, unsatiated by gaining resources and territory. They possessed inherent cruelty, enjoying our suffering and engaging in behavior solely to cause us pain."

Khali looked the male representation up and down. "Cruelty . . . like the needless destruction of Jya?"

"Exactly. The war with them had ended. The Shandi had been defeated. They did it as punishment. Their cruelty outweighed their greed, for Jya was a paradise, lush with resources they could have exploited."

Khali considered for a moment then asked, "What are the primary lessons of the Mak'Tar?"

"We had never encountered such evil before. Irivat and The First had become slaves to the Mak'Tar, reduced to physical laborers in a cruel environment—insignificant to their masters. He heard of the destruction of Jya and the imminent defeat of our people.

"Irivat led the revolt to overthrow their slave masters. Their actions were bold and unexpected. They seized their master's ships and proceeded to the next colony, cascading throughout the Mak'Tar empire.

"For the survival of the Shandi, they surrendered to their mission. To their duty. There was no self. There was only the Shandi. These are the virtues of our society today.

"They placed their duty to the Shandi over everything else. They worked tirelessly, in continuous rotation, as we do now. Their dedication and resolve rewarded them with victory after victory, cutting through the Mak'Tar colonies and eventually their entire fleet. The Mak'Tar were not prepared for such an onslaught, especially not from the defeated Shandi. Still, our enemy fought to the last and, eventually, faded from existence."

Khali interrupted, "Irivat had a daughter. Did he not?"

Maya sighed then produced a flat smile. "Yes. Of course. His daughter. Born into slavery and raised during the war. She became the most revered leader in the history of the Shandi."

Khali smiled. "Her name was also Khali."

"Yes, Khali, it was. I hope you strive to be equal to your namesake." Her mother raised her brows. "The lesson of the Mak'Tar is to remain dutiful and diligent. You must submit to your station. There is no self—only the Shandi. A society dedicated to purpose and devoted to their duty can prevail against anything, even an unthinkable evil."

Khali deeply studied the visuals of the Mak'Tar people. Their harmless depiction paled in comparison to what she had seen in her nightmares. How could something seemingly benign be so malevolent? "What should I focus on here?"

"All of it," Maya said. "Retain every aspect of their behavior. They are the most dangerous race we have ever encountered. We will never meet them again, but we may meet something similar."

"Vimati says to never say never. Expect the unexpected," Khali said.

"It is more likely that we encounter something worse. Some other type of—monster."

Khali reviewed the readouts to see if she had any more questions. A shiver ran down her spine as she repeated quietly to herself, "Monster."

Made in the USA
Las Vegas, NV
16 February 2024

85881044R00085